Mariposa b

D0191782

DISCARDED

"You and I've always been on the same side, but not last night, for damn sure, and not anymore since you're gonna work for Mitch."

"If I'm going to be around Pepperoni, I have to work for Mitch."

"Is Mitch gonna pay you?"

"Well, sure, but—"

"Well, don't gamble it all away. Give your mom some. Let her put it in the bank."

My voice was clear and hard, and for once it didn't threaten to break. "When Mitch pays me, it's my money. I can do what I want with it."

His eyes went to slits, and I knew he was grinding his teeth. In spite of myself, I took a step back, then another. Then he just shook his head.

"I give up," he said, stalking away...

"The plot is tight and the characters well-drawn. Add to that some first-rate confrontational scenes between dad and son and a generous infusion of humor—Koertge's particularly adept at one-line comebacks—and you wind up with a thoroughly good read." *Booklist*

East Union High School
Library
Manteca Unified School District

"A well-crafted, wholly believable picture of a boy in transition."

Kirkus (Pointered Review)

"Fast paced, full of appealing themes, entertaining...with characters that are believable."

The ALAN Review

Other Avon Flare Books by
Ron Koertge

THE ARIZONA KID
THE BOY IN THE MOON
WHERE THE KISSING NEVER STOPS

Avon Books are available at special quantity discounts for bulk purchases for sales promotions, premiums, fund raising or educational use. Special books, or book excerpts, can also be created to fit specific needs.

For details write or telephone the office of the Director of Special Markets, Avon Books, Dept. FP, 1350 Avenue of the Americas, New York, New York 10019, 1-800-238-0658.

RON KOERTGE

AN AVON FLARE BOOK

If you purchased this book without a cover, you should be aware that this book is stolen property. It was reported as "unsold and destroyed" to the publisher, and neither the author nor the publisher has received any payment for this "stripped book."

For bianca, with love.
And in memory of the great filly Ruffian,
who broke down during her match race
with Foolish Pleasure, July 6, 1975.

The characters and events portrayed in this book are fictitious. Any similarity to real persons, living or dead, is coincidental and not intended by the author.

AVON BOOKS
A division of
The Hearst Corporation
1350 Avenue of the Americas
New York, New York 10019

"A Joy Street Book"
Copyright © 1991 by Ronald Koertge
Published by arrangement with Little, Brown and Company
Library of Congress Catalog Card Number: 90-20730
ISBN: 0-380-71761-1
RL: 5.5

All rights reserved, which includes the right to reproduce this book or portions thereof in any form whatsoever except as provided by the U.S. Copyright Law. For information address Little, Brown and Company, 34 Beacon Street, Boston, Massachusetts 02108.

First Avon Flare Printing: March 1993

AVON FLARE TRADEMARK REG. U.S. PAT. OFF. AND IN OTHER COUNTRIES, MARCA REGISTRADA, HECHO EN U.S.A.

Printed in the U.S.A.

RA   10   9   8   7   6   5   4   3   2   1

PART ONE

=While Dad rode around checking the other horses, I just sat on Pepperoni and looked out at the ocean. *Stared* out at the ocean, actually. And wondered why I wasn't as happy doing this as I'd been last year, and the year before that, and the year before that.

The filly stood way past her knees in the cool, salty water, and every now and then she'd lean her head down and nose around in the frothy shore break.

A bridle was the only tack she ever needed when I rode her, and I let the reins droop. She'd do what I wanted anyway if I just asked, and sometimes she'd do it if I only *thought* about asking.

When my dad motioned for the exercise boys and the grooms to head for the backstretch, I leaned and put my cheek against her stiff, shiny mane,

"Listen, girl," I said, "I feel a little weird this summer, but it's got nothin' to do with you, okay? You look great, like a real race horse."

Then I sat up and tugged at my hat.

"Graham!" Dad's voice was faint. "Hurry up!"

"Yes, sir," I said, mostly to myself. "Of course, sir. Whatever you say, sir."

Maybe he was right. What was the delay, anyhow? I'd talked to Pepperoni all her life, but this was the first time I ever waited for an answer.

Jeez, maybe I was in worse shape than I thought!

≡ ≡ ≡

Just about noon, I threw my mountain bike against the side of the condo and stalked up the stairs, kicking a new green boogie board out of the way. My cowboy boots felt as big as Frankenstein's shoes, and the heavy leather chaps wrapped themselves around my legs like giant kelp pods.

Inside, Mom — dressed in shiny blue running pants and a Nike T-shirt — was tinkering with a machine that made juice out of anything. Boxes were stacked all around with big Magic Marker labels on them: PUT THIS AWAY FIRST, NECESSARY JUNK, JUST PLAIN JUNK.

"Hi," she said without turning around.

I started hopping on one foot, tugging at my left boot. When that didn't work, I gave up and went after the buckles on my chaps.

"I hate this stuff!" I announced.

Mom turned around. She put a white plastic funnel to one eye and squinted through it at me.

"What stuff?"

I held up one foot. "This stuff."

"Really?" she asked. "I think you look great. Your dad was wearing boots the night we met."

"Yeah, but he wasn't riding a little, shrimpy bicycle and some big guys didn't yell, 'Hey, dude. Get a horse!'"

"Is that all?" She pushed PUT THIS AWAY FIRST out of the way and reached for NECESSARY JUNK. "Graham, they were just kids."

"Mom, *I'm* just a kid," I pointed out.

"Hmmm." Which meant I'm-listening-but-not-seriously. "Why'd you wear your chaps home, anyway? You usually —"

"I was thinking, okay? I had stuff on my mind."

"A lot of deep thinkers wear chaps. I saw a picture of Einstein once, and he was wearing them."

I knew if I grinned my crappy mood would burn away like cellophane in fire. But I didn't grin. Or couldn't. Or wouldn't.

I sat down, wrestled my Justins off, and started in on the last silver buckle of my black leather chaps. *Black leather,* I thought. *Who are you kidding, Graham? You don't look cool. You look like the Lone Moron.*

"Next Christmas, I don't want presents. I just want money."

"Christmas? Graham, it's only June."

"Yeah, well, I want to buy all new clothes. And I want to go pick 'em out myself."

5

"For now," Mom said, frowning down the snout of her juicer, "just hang those chaps over by the door, and I'll take them down to the barns later on."

I stood up and hurled them into the corner.

My mother turned around then and got that look that meant she was about to put the back of her hand on my forehead.

"Are you okay?"

"Yes," I lied. Then, not wanting to worry her, I added another half-lie. "Maybe I'm just disappointed. Leslie said she'd be here this morning."

"When was that?"

"Last time I talked to her, just before we left L.A."

Mom nodded. "It's probably not her fault. You know Mitch."

I did know Mitch. He might've called the horse van company so late he couldn't get space. He might've stayed in San Francisco one more day. Or stopped at one of the off-track betting places and got too hot to leave. Or swung around by Chino to look at some yearlings.

Anyway, as I sat back in the red canvas director's chair by the kitchen table, I thought that maybe what I'd said wasn't so much half a lie as just not the whole truth. I *did* want to see Leslie, but that wasn't all of it. I'd been hoping Mariposa would make a difference, that it would be the magic place it'd been every summer for as long as I could remember, and now I was afraid it wasn't.

Instead, I felt the same as I had back home. Whatever was bothering me, I hadn't left it behind.

Even sitting on Pepperoni I'd thought, *I'd like to be surfing*, but the minute I did I also thought, *And if you were surfing, you'd want to be doing this.* And I knew that was true, too. No wonder I'd forgottten to take my chaps off when I was through on the backstretch: I wasn't thinking, or maybe I was thinking too much.

Just then Mom said, "I saw you about nine o'clock when I was jogging. I waved."

"I've been a little out of it today."

She smiled to herself, her green eyes narrowing. "I love to see beautiful horses up to their bellies in the ocean. When your dad and I were just starting out and we only had Perkins Palace, Mystery Horse, and Little Bows, that was the part of coming to Mariposa I liked best. Just sitting out there with those fillies."

The minute she said it, I knew she was right. And then I missed feeling that way, which just about made me cry, for God's sake. My emotions were just wrecked lately. Back and forth. Up and down. In fact, my whole life reminded me of one of those rides at Magic Mountain that turn you every way but loose. Except that there was no safety bar clamped down on my knees. And I didn't know — not anymore, anyway — exactly where I'd be once I staggered off.

Just then, Mom ran both hands through her red hair — cut sleek and swept back at the sides for summer — then wiped them on her shirt before she plugged her juicer in, flipped a switch, and began to feed it from a green bowl with flowers on the side. I watched something gray ooze out of the end.

In a minute or two she held out half a glassful, but I made the two-fingered sign of the cross that always works in Dracula movies.

"What vegetable is gray?" I asked. "That stuff looks like Fluffy."

"Don't worry, Grandma is keeping Fluffy while we're gone. This is potatoes and beets. In a few weeks I won't have a toxic cell in my body."

I shook my head. "Well, I think old toxic me will go surf for a while, okay?"

"I'll tell you what." She fed the machine another potato. "I'll trade you."

I stopped halfway to the stairs. "Trade me what for what?"

"You can go surfing if you tell me why you got a C in math."

Uh-oh. "My grades came."

She leaned against the sink. "The mailman had a black band around one arm, and he was followed by a small band of mourners."

"Mom. One C. In my whole life, one C."

"Was math too hard?"

"Do you want the truth?"

"Please."

"It was too easy."

She took a sip of juice, holding it in her mouth a second like she was tasting wine. Then she said, "Okay."

"Okay what?"

"Okay you can go surfing."

"That's it?"

"I said if you'd tell me you could go, and you told me." She leaned toward the ocean not a hundred yards away. "So surf already. Try your new board."

Suddenly I felt like such a creep. My parents had just bought me a great new Linden to replace my thrashed McCoy. And what do I do? Get a C in math. And what does my mom do? Ask me one simple question, then tell me to have a good time.

"Mom?"

She was putting frozen pizza crusts into the freezer. "Hmm."

"Thanks for the board." It was the best I could do.

≡ ≡ ≡

A couple of minutes later I came downstairs in my SideOut trunks and a tank top. Mom was putting things away at top speed by then, so I had to move around just to stay out of the way.

"Let me help," I said finally.

"No, I'm fine. You go on."

"I want to. Really."

"Well, then lift those boxes, okay?" She pointed to a couple of cartons in a far corner, then patted the table. "Just put them up here."

I squatted the way Dad had shown me, and lifted with my legs, not my back. The boxes were pretty heavy, but I tried to make it look easy.

Mom said, "You're stronger than last year."

"I guess."

"You're probably stronger than last month." She narrowed her eyes as if we were at the horse pavilion in Keenland and she was about to bid on something. "Your whole body is different."

That embarrassed me, because she didn't really know how different. Or where. "My feet are huge," I said quickly. "Maybe I should switch from surfing to water-skiing." I held up one size ten. "I've got most of the equipment built-in."

"I'll bet you're going to be taller than your dad."

That was hard to imagine — looking my father right in the eye or, even better, looking down at him.

Suddenly I yawned.

"Sea air?" Mom asked with a smile.

"I guess I'm not used to getting up at five-thirty every morning."

"Your dad's a tank, isn't he? Rain or shine, sick or well, he's down there at the barns."

I wondered if I could do that. I wondered if I wanted to.

Mom reached for her car keys. "I've got to run an errand. I won't be gone long."

I'd been teetering on one foot sort of like a heron,

when I slipped, banged my knee good, and reached for the wall to catch myself.

"You okay?" Mom asked automatically.

"Fine. I'm fine." I hobbled toward the door. "Just lost my balance."

"Dad said if you surf, be sure and check the lifeguard flags. There's some big hurricane in Baja."

"I'm not a complete idiot, Mom. And I sure don't need Dad to tell me how to surf. He doesn't know squat about the ocean." Then I was gone before she could tell me to cool it. Or I thought I was.

All of a sudden she was out on the deck. She wasn't yelling, exactly, but her voice sure carried: "Graham, this is my vacation, too. You ruin it for me by being crabby all the time and we're gonna have a long talk real soon."

I crossed the Pacific Coast Highway and hiked down toward the water, winding my way through people with coolers, huge umbrellas, and paperbacks. Then I slipped the tether around my ankle and waded in.

It was always a shock to hit the water, but I always liked it. Surfing got me out of my head and into my body, and I started to do the necessary stuff naturally: paddling out face down through the soup, going up and over the waves with other surfers stacked on them, and finally scoping out the next set. All pretty much automatically, trusting my body to do it and to get it right.

Not thinking it through the way I did my dry life. Not wondering all the time.

As I waited out there, straddling my board, keeping the tip tilted up, just for fun I tried to think through the things I'd taught myself to do automatically. *So, okay, here comes a wave. Let's see now. I'll swing around, face the shore, slide back just a . . .*

Big surprise — I missed it. While the guy beside me just shot to his feet and was gone. So next time I let my body do the thinking and left the calculations to the parts of me that I could just trust to do the right thing. Sure enough: at the precise right second, I caught the crest, stood up, inched forward just enough, and angled across the face of a very nice five-footer. My feet were like a blind person's hands — they knew.

Then, my knees bent a little, my butt tucked under, I dropped one shoulder a notch, glided through the last part, kicked out nice, and dropped back onto my board, pointing west, ready to do it again.

Yeah — balance was what did it. Balance I seemed to never have on dry land.

≡ ≡ ≡

A few hours later, I was swimming again, but not in the ocean. I was swimming up from sleep, seeing — just like I did when I fell off my board and got shoved down toward the bottom — the light somewhere above me.

My mom knocked softly. "It's almost suppertime, Graham. Can I come in?"

I grunted and pulled the covers over me. I'd started to feel funny about her seeing me in my underwear.

"I guess I fell asleep." I sat up, tugged at the blue bedspread, and glanced around at the unfamiliar walls. One of the renters before us had turned the room into a nursery. Happy lambs bounced over tiny fences, and smiling cows stared down at me. Mom came over and sat on the edge of the bed.

"It's too weird in here," I said, sounding grumpy. "All these happy little animals. What a joke. We kill those guys for dinner."

"When I talked to the realtor I tried to get us one of the units with vegetarian wallpaper, but they'd all been snapped up."

I couldn't help but grin a little. Then I yawned and said, "Surfing down here was harder than I remembered. I really had to work to get outside."

"How's the new board?"

"It's great." I pawed at my hair, which was not red like Mom's but dark like my dad's. Not straight like hers but springy and tight like his.

It was safe to stand up in my underwear by then, so I tumbled out and halfheartedly picked up a few piles of clothes and moved them somewhere else. "How long did I sleep?"

"Years, Mr. van Winkle. The whole town has changed. Only I have remained young and beautiful." I watched her rub the red marks her glasses made on her nose.

"Were you working?"

"Uh-huh. Mostly getting my computer back together and talking to Mr. Christie in London. I think we're going to buy that Lyphard colt. Dad showed you his picture, remember? Big roan, looks like he could run forever?"

"He's not as big as Pepperoni."

"Thank goodness. I just paid the feed bills." Then she stretched and stood up. I could see something tucked inside the back pocket of her jeans.

"What's that?"

She showed me. "A Twinkie."

"Why are you sitting on a Twinkie?"

"It's to remind me that if I eat it, that's where it'll go." She inhaled and tucked it away. "I'm making something nice for you and your dad. I, on the other hand, am having primordial ooze."

Every summer Mom ate this concoction called Beiler's Broth made from green beans, parsley, zucchini, and celery. It was completely green and primitive looking. I always thought that if you just left it out by itself in the sun for a little while, something would crawl out, take a big breath, and start worshipping fire.

"Get cleaned up, okay?" she said from the door. "We'll eat in just a minute."

I was starved, so I pulled on a clean T-shirt and some baggies, splashed water toward my face, and hurried downstairs. A little too fast, too, because right at the bottom I caught my foot on something and fell the last step and a half.

"Shit!" I said, rubbing my knee.

I felt my dad glance at me over the top of his racing form. All I could really see was his hairline, which was receding on both sides. So *it* frowned.

I stood up and gingerly tried my leg. "All right, all right. But you say worse a hundred times a day."

"That doesn't mean I want to hear you say it. And it's not a hundred."

"What's the difference? It's a lot." I pulled my chair out hard. "And I don't see why it's okay for you but not okay for me. It's like I don't have any rights."

"There's two reasons, really. First of all, you don't do it very well."

"Do what, swear?"

"That's right. You're not good at it yet."

"Who has to be good?"

"If you want to swear around me, you do. You don't have the feel for it. If we were talkin' about Spanish, right now you sound like you learned it by mail. You know how I am: I want nothing to do with the second-rate. I don't hold it against you for wanting to practice, but I don't want you to practice around me. It hurts my ears."

"What's the second reason?"

"Let's just leave it at that and eat, okay?"

"No, tell me."

"Graham, you're not even fourteen, so you have to do pretty much what your mom and I say."

I looked at my mother.

"He's right, sweetheart. A year, maybe two," she said, "and you'll be good enough to go out on your own and swear for a living, but not yet."

Dad smiled, mostly to himself, and reached for the plate of garlic toast.

"This isn't funny."

"Maybe not," Dad said, "but it's nothin' to dial 911 about, either."

"It's just horrible to think I'm stuck like this. I'm no better than those horses down there."

Dad held out his plate, and Mom gave him a huge helping of spaghetti. "You've just run smack up against the limits, that's all," he said. "Everybody's got 'em, and nobody likes to think about 'em very much."

"You don't have limits."

"Oh, no? Any owner can call me up any time of the day or night, and I have to talk to him."

"You don't do what they want, though."

"And how would you know that? You're at school or ridin' your surfboard or playing baseball." He picked up his fork. "Everybody makes compromises and then shuts up about what can't be changed."

"Meaning you want me to shut up."

"I'm hungry. I've been up since five, and I've got more sore horses now than when I shipped down here. How they got sore ridin' in a van is beyond me."

Mom stirred her bowl of green broth, added curry powder, and asked, "Who's sore now?"

The talk turned, as it always did, to horses — how they looked and felt, galloped and stood, acted, ate, slept, lathered up, and cooled out.

I was still mad, so I kept both elbows on the table and, with my face real close to the plate, just shoveled the food in: all stuff Mom and Dad hated. But they just acted like I wasn't there, and pretty soon I got about half sick to my stomach and stopped.

Anyway, I was interested. I didn't want to be, but I was. They were talking about Vital Signs, Lilting Line of Bach, The Doctor Ordered, and American Poetry, the best turf horses Dad trained. *And* they were talking about Pepperoni, my favorite, almost my horse. She was the biggest two-year-old anybody had ever seen, maybe the biggest two-year-old in the world.

So I sat up straight, put one hand in my lap, and wiped my mouth with a napkin.

"Could you work Pepperoni a mile some morning?"

He shrugged. "I don't see why not."

"When?"

When he looked right at me, I sat up even straighter: the perfect kid.

"I keep thinking I will, but then I don't. I'm waiting for . . ." He glanced at Mom.

17

"An irresistible impulse?" she suggested.

He smiled across at her. "Something like that."

Mom scraped the last spoonful out of her bowl. If I listened hard, I could hear the ocean.

"Do you ever get tired of this?" I asked. "I mean every morning . . ."

"Mornings are best for me, son. You know that. Mornings down here, especially."

"Yeah, but . . ."

They were both looking at me. Mom tried to jump-start me. "But . . ."

"Nothing, I guess."

Ten minutes later I was helping clear the table as my dad took a big breath and let it out. "God bless Mariposa," he said, mostly to himself. "I work just as hard down here, but it feels different."

He laced both hands across his stomach, looking contented. He wasn't just heavy; he was strong, too. Really strong. I'd seen him lean into a yearling that was almost too sick to stand up and just heave her into a corner where she could rest. I couldn't imagine I'd ever be like that.

"Did you tell your mom what management did to the backstretch, Graham?"

"No, I was . . ."

He turned in his chair. "They reroofed a couple of the barns, honey, and spiffed things up."

Then he took a sip of iced tea from a glass decorated with sea horses and slapped my butt pretty hard as I went past. "You know, it's probably unlucky to talk about this, but we could have a good meet. A great one if everything goes right."

We. Not just him and Mom. Not just the people who worked for him down at the barns. Not just the owners he trained for. But him and me, too. Ever since I was old enough to understand, I'd loved it when he said *we*, meaning the two of us. We'll do this, we'll go here, we'll run this horse a week from tomorrow. Now I stood there only half-listening.

As I bent over the table with a damp dishrag, he asked, "Are you okay, son?"

"Yes, sir."

"You look kind of worried."

"I was wondering if Leslie'd come in yet." What a handy half-lie that was.

"Mitch is always a day late and a dollar short, but he usually gets here." Dad stood up and adjusted the big brass buckle that poked him in the belly. "Probably he'll show up just about the time we do the night inspection."

"Well," I said, putting the rag down and staring at it, "I'll, uh, just meet you over there."

"Over where?"

I couldn't seem to look right at him. I followed the squiggly pattern of the wallpaper. "At the, uh, barns. I'll meet you there. I'll take my bike."

I felt him studying me. "You don't want to ride with me?"

"I just . . . well, you know, I haven't seen the town

in nine months. I just thought I'd prowl around a little on my own."

He nodded, unconvinced, as Mom brought two steaming cups of coffee to the table. Then he looked over at her, grinned, and pointed to his forehead.

"Maybe he's the reason I'm losin' my hair!"

≡ ≡ ≡

Halfway to the track, on top of the biggest hill, I stopped to get my breath and to zip up my red sweatshirt. It had CALIFORNIA written all up and down one sleeve, and I looked at it and frowned. Was I too dense to remember what state this was?

From up there, the town didn't look real: twinkling lights, shimmering ocean, white houses, a factory with trucks lined up beside each other, the red crossing lights at the corner of Balboa and Beach. It reminded me of those towns that kids who are crazy about trains build. And I could've been an accessory by Lionel — Kid on Bike — something that did the same thing every time the switch was thrown.

So was I like some pathetic little toy that lit up whenever Dad threw the switch? My pounding heart said yes then no then yes then no. I needed to talk to Leslie, so I started out again, crossing my fingers, hoping she'd be there.

At the foot of the hill, I coasted over the railroad tracks that separated the rich part of town from the poor part. My dad liked it that the races were held on the so-called wrong side of the tracks. He said it reminded him of the old days when horse racing had a kind of bad reputation. Or if not bad, then at least rough-and-tumble. In the fifteen years he'd been training thoroughbreds, he'd seen it change from an interesting and pretty unconventional way to make a living into a business — a *big* business.

Dad had pointed out guys on the backstretch now who were there just for the money, not because they loved it or even liked it very much. They got degrees in equine science; they had graphs with curves on them and dots that stood for horses, dots with names like vitamins: B1, B2, B12.

My dad, though, walked around and looked at his stock, undid the webbing in front of every stall, strolled in, and put his hands on a leg or a hip. He talked to horses, hunkered down and rewrapped a bandage, reached into a trough and got his hand wet picking out some loose straw. He was the hands-on part of the business. Mom and her computer took care of the rest.

I glided down the last incline and right up to the stable gate. Then I got off and pushed my bike through because horses don't like things that go whirr in the dark.

"Hold it right there now!"

I turned as a big guy came out of the guard's shack. "And where might you be going?" he asked.

"Just back to my dad's barn."

"And he is?"

East Union High School Library 940095
Manteca Unified School District

"John Carpenter."

As he checked a clipboard, he tugged at his hat. It had a little, shiny bill like a bus driver's cap. "Mr. Carpenter just came through here not ten minutes ago."

"I know that. I'm going to meet him."

"If you're his son, why didn't you ride in with him?"

I looked up at the big, suspicious face. "Because I didn't want to. I wanted to come on my bike. By myself. What are you thinking — that I'm a clever band of horse thieves disguised as a thirteen-year-old kid?"

"Don't start on me with an attitude now, son. I've got one at home a little older than you, and he's wearing an earring."

"What's that supposed to mean?"

He held out a big, empty hand. "Let's see some ID."

"Everybody knows me. You're the stranger around here."

"What's the problem, Alex?"

Another guard had walked up while we were arguing. This one looked familiar. "You know me, don't you, Tony?" I asked, reading his name tag.

"Sure. You're John Carpenter's kid."

"See?"

The first guard put both hands on his hips. "How am I supposed to know that?" he grumbled.

"You know his dad, don't you?"

"Yeah, so?"

Tony glanced down at me. "Well, he looks just like him."

22

East Union High School
Library

I told him I wasn't so sure of that. "Sort of like him, maybe, but not just."

"Are you kidding? You look exactly like him."

It seemed like I'd heard that forever — two of a kind or chip off the old block or spittin' image. Maybe that's why I started to yell, "I don't either! He's taller than I am. He weighs more. We don't think the same. I'm not as strong, and I don't wear a hat like his or walk like him or even wear his after-shave because I don't shave at all much less shave just like he does." I'd lost it again. Just like at dinner.

Tony started to nod his head. He sucked his teeth real loud and hooked one thumb in his gun belt. "Okay, Graham. Have it your way. I never saw you before, you look like nobody I've ever seen, and from now on you'd better wear your credentials or you'll be sittin' home with your momma, who I don't know either."

I was almost to our barns when I saw Mitch's old pickup with TEQUILA SUNRISE RANCH painted on the door. He'd bought that Chevy one Friday after he'd drunk a bunch of tequila sunrises and won a bunch of money. There wasn't really a ranch, but he'd always planned to win a whole lot more someday and buy one and give it that name.

Slowing down a little, I took a deep breath. I loved it on the backstretch. It was cool and peaceful, and it smelled good, like healthy animals, clean straw, and fresh alfalfa. It's one of the first odors I remember — not milk or cookies, but the smell of a stable.

Then I came around a corner, and there they all were: Mitch, leaning in the door to his office, smoking and smiling, as always a kind of crooked half-smile. Donna with her faded T-shirt saying LET'S HORSE AROUND. And Leslie with a new sky-high hairdo, standing with both arms out like she was on a rope twenty feet off the ground.

Donna was coaching her. "Just walk, honey. It'll take care of itself."

Leslie put her hands up so the long sleeves of a red, silky-looking blouse slid down her tanned forearms. "It feels like it's gonna slip!"

"Act natural!" Donna advised. "Let the boys look at your hair. You're composed. You're in control."

Leslie yelled, "This thing's heavy, Donna."

"No, it's not!" she bellowed. "It's a versatile style that can be professional in the daytime and carefree in the evening."

"I don't want to be professional in the daytime."

Just then the phone rang, and Mitch, who'd moved to a bench, yelled for Donna to get it. She set off at a dead run, then pulled herself up short, like a cutting horse.

"You're closer to the phone, Mitch."

He slid down the bench a yard or so. "Not anymore."

So Donna backed up a few yards. "Now who's closest?"

Mitch grinned, stood up, and strolled backward into the office, keeping his eyes on Donna the whole time.

I stepped out of the shadows. "Hey," I said. "Where've you been?"

"Graham!" Leslie ran toward me, put both hands up, and we did a double high five, a hard one that made my palms sting and shook all that piled-up hair loose so it tumbled forward into her eyes.

"Shit!" she said.

"Don't let my dad hear you say that."

She marched to the nearest faucet, kicked a bucket out of the way, and turned the tap; it came on with a whoosh, and Leslie stuck her head under it and started to wash her hair with half a bar of Fels Naptha that was lying there.

Bent over like she was, I could see down her blouse, all the way to where her white bra started. I looked away so fast I could feel it in my neck.

"That better?" she asked, standing up and wringing her hair out into a ponytail.

"Yeah," I answered, meaning about ten things at once. Then I asked, "Is Donna working with you guys now? I never got any free hair advice when she was working for us."

"You were lucky!" Leslie toned it down a little and pulled me closer. "Don't get me wrong — she works hard, but she and Dad have a kind of thing, too."

"So that's why they were playing who's-closer-to-the-phone." I shook my head. "It's weird to see grown-ups do stuff like that, isn't it?"

"And kind of sickening." Then she put one arm

through mine and dragged me toward a bench. "Well, tell me everything."

"You tell me. I wrote a lot. You're the one didn't write back."

"Not much to tell. Dad said the track up there had too much sand in it and all his horses have big feet and couldn't take hold. So we're down here now. And then back to L.A."

"I meant what happened to *you*."

A shrug. A look away. "Worked at the track. Went to school. Did crummy." Back to me. "You get all A's again?"

"C in math."

"You're kidding."

"Don't sound so glad."

Just then Mitch leaned out the office door, holding on with one arm like a train conductor. "Leslie!" he yelled. "What's that new horse's name?"

"He's in the fourth or fifth stall down."

"I know *where* he is. I want to know *who* he is."

"Ask Donna."

"She said to ask you." *Bam!* went the door.

Leslie shrugged and grinned. "Remember," she said, "when you stood up in class that day and knew the names of all the presidents in order?"

"That was a trick. Dad taught me."

"I could never have learned those."

"You wouldn't listen when I tried to tell you how."

"What's the difference? I couldn't learn it."

She leaned over and wrung out her hair one last time. I kept my eyes down, watching the drops fall.

"New boots?" I asked.

"Yeah." She stuck one out and admired it. "Red."

"No kidding."

"I kind of wanted a different look this summer." She touched her wet hair. "But not that different."

I checked for Donna or Mitch, then slid closer. "Speaking of looks," I said, "you don't think I look just like my dad, do you?"

"Sure."

"Not *just* like."

"Well, maybe not *just* like, but . . ."

"I know we're related and all that, but I'm not some transistorized version of him, am I?"

She leaned back and narrowed her gray eyes. "You're taller than the last time I saw you."

"Is that all?"

She shrugged. "Probably you feel different inside."

She didn't know how true that was. But I said, "I guess I was just thinking that you're not all that much like Mitch."

"What's wrong with Mitch?"

"Nothing's wrong with him. I just mean that you're who you are. You're yourself."

She looked suspicious. "So?"

"Well, do you think I'm myself?"

She eyed me curiously. "Who else would you be?"

We weren't that far away from Dad's barns, and I heard one of the stallions whinny.

"Well, whoever I am, I better get over there."

"I'll walk partway."

Neither of us said anything for a few seconds. Then a mare started up a long way off, and the stallion answered, kicking the back of his stall for good measure.

Suddenly Leslie jammed both hands in her back pockets and started to take big, sweeping steps like she was skating. I hurried to keep up.

"Graham? Do you think animals have thoughts?"

"Sure. Like 'When's dinner?' and 'Don't pull that cinch too tight.'"

"Not regular thoughts. Other kinds."

"What other kinds?"

She stopped skating so fast I almost bumped into her. Then she put both arms out like a dancer and tried to spin around. "You know. Sexy thoughts."

"Gee, Leslie. I don't know."

"Sure you do. You read all the time."

"Not about that."

"Then make an educated guess."

She looked at me, and I looked away. Then I looked at her, and she looked away.

"Well, they mate, but that's probably an instinct."

"Okay, but do they think first? Are they curious? Do they get scared?"

"I guess," I said, "they just do it. I mean like people, but not like people."

She blotted her forehead with one sleeve. I was warm, too.

Leslie tugged at my shirt, and we stopped. "Remember Mr. DiFiero's place?" she whispered.

I looked around. "Sure."

Leslie frowned. "Not the whole ranch, Graham. Part of it."

"Which part?"

She looked exasperated. "Where they breed the horses."

"Oh, yeah. That." Our folks hadn't let us inside, but we knew what was going on.

"The mare went right in," Leslie said. "She seemed to want to."

"Maybe they'd exchanged class pictures. Or talked on the phone."

Leslie snickered. "It seemed so crude."

"Yeah. He didn't even take her downtown to see *Return of the Black Stallion* first."

That just put her away. Me, too, actually: two big horses sitting up in the dark holding hooves and sharing a box of hot buttered hay.

We were snorting and spitting, hands clamped over our mouths, making those pig sounds that always come out when you try not to laugh out loud. But we weren't doing too good. I heard horses stirring all around us.

And then I saw my dad come around the corner with his teeth clenched.

"Unbelievable," he said, looming over us. "I was gonna fire somebody, and instead it's a couple of kids I have to keep no matter what."

Leslie stared down at her boots. "I'm sorry, Mr. Carpenter."

"You should be, Leslie. You know better."

"Yes, sir."

Then it was my turn. "And what's the matter with you, Graham?"

"I don't know."

"Look at me when you talk."

I glared up. "I don't know," I said slowly.

"What kind of answer is that?"

"What kind of question is it? I haven't seen Leslie in a long time. We were just talking."

"You were talking too loud."

"All right. I know that. I apologize."

But he was fuming. "I've been walking around on eggs so that roan filly would just lay down a little while, and I no more than get it done when you two yahoos come along and scare her. Now if she don't run, Graham, where am I supposed to get the money to buy you surfboards and —"

"Hold it, Dad." I held up both hands. "Don't buy me things, okay, if you don't want to, and don't act like Leslie and I just ruined your chances to win the Kentucky Derby. We said we were sorry. We'll have corrective humor surgery. We'll never laugh again."

Without raising her head much, Leslie glanced at me sideways. A vein in my dad's forehead was pounding. He took two or three deep breaths. Leslie slid her right boot over and bumped my left one.

"Where were you, anyway?" Dad asked once he'd cooled down a little. "I wanted you to hold Pepperoni for me."

"Why, what's wrong?

"Nothing's wrong. She's just full of herself, and when she's like that you're the only one she'll settle down for."

"Well, let's do it now."

"I did it myself, but I didn't like it. She about ate my lunch. Damn it, Graham, I thought we were gonna do rounds together."

I looked up at him again. "Dad, I don't do anything except trail along after you."

"Sure you do."

"Really? What?"

He rubbed his face with the heel of one hand. I could hear his beard rasp. "It just helps to have you there. I need somebody to talk to."

"You don't talk to me; you talk to yourself. Then you go back and write everything on the chalkboard for the next morning."

"Maybe, but it's easier if you're there."

I pointed to the little rooms where some of the grooms slept. "Use Victor."

"Victor doesn't listen."

"Dad, I don't listen sometimes."

"Sure you do, Graham."

We were past the office by that time, headed down shed row. Leslie slowed up and hooked one finger in my back pocket.

"I gotta go," she said, tugging at me.

Dad turned, too. "Have you seen Pepperoni?"

She shook her head, eyes still down. "I will though. Tomorrow maybe."

"She's still growin'."

Finally Leslie looked up at him. "You're kidding."

Dad shook his head and smiled. A little. "We're gonna need a stall with a sunroof if this keeps up."

I asked if we could go back. "We'll be quiet."

"All right. And check on Beaufort Wants To Know while you're there. He didn't eat up too good last time."

We crept through the long, dim barn. Most of the runners were asleep or at least resting. Horses really can sleep standing up, but not all of them do.

We could see Pepperoni's big head sticking out of the stall.

"She's awake," said Leslie.

When she saw us, she started to nod and make that fluttery *brrrrrr* sound. Leslie made sure Pepperoni knew who she was. The last thing we needed was for this huge filly to rear up in her stall.

"Hi, girl," she said softly.

Pepperoni turned her head a little, then shuffled forward.

Leslie rubbed Pepperoni's big, black nose, which had a dozen or so hairs growing out of it. "How can she keep growing?" she asked.

"She's not growing anymore. She's done."

"Your dad said . . ."

"I know, but she won't get any bigger now."

Leslie turned to me. "How do you know?"

I shrugged. "I just know."

Leslie cocked her head. "Well, if anybody does, you do." Leslie checked behind her to make sure we were alone. Then she said, "It's cool that your dad can't handle her sometimes, but you can."

Just then Pepperoni angled toward me. I looked up so she could nibble my hair. Then I put my arms as far around her big neck as I could.

"Do you think," Leslie asked, "that you'll ever have a girlfriend?"

"I guess so, sometime. Why?"

"Because nothing and nobody makes you as happy as this horse."

"I'll probably just get me a tall girlfriend who wears steel shoes."

"See? You're in a better mood already."

I usually did feel good around Pepperoni, and we really were close. I was right there at Mr. DiFiero's ranch when she was born. I'd named her, helped nurse

33

her through a really bad case of colic, watched her grow, grown with her. Except for Leslie, she was my best friend.

Leslie stepped back and shook her head admiringly. "She looks great. Is she workin' good?"

I glanced around, then pulled Leslie closer. "More than that. She *wants* to run. I know she could win if Dad would just find her a race that's long enough."

We looked at each other and grinned, picturing us down in the winner's circle with Pepperoni while she posed for pictures after breaking the track record.

"God, she could be a champion," said Leslie.

"All she needs is the chance."

Pepperoni turned around and took a mouthful of hay.

"Maybe she'd sleep if we left her alone," I said. "Let me take a look at old Beaufort Wants To Know, and then we'll get out of here."

When we rounded the corner near the office a few minutes later, Mitch saw us first, leaned toward Dad, and said something. Then he laughed and slapped his leg. My father smiled.

"Hi, Graham," Mitch said, holding out his hand. "You look more like your dad every day."

"Then how can you be sure it's really me and not just one of the many clones he keeps around so he has somebody to talk at?"

Mitch cocked his head for a second as if what I'd said actually registered, but then it was gone. If you ask me, grown-ups almost never listen to kids. We're just the sound of surf in the background. White noise.

Mitch turned to Leslie. "You ready, sugar?"

"Whenever." Then she turned to me. "See you tomorrow, okay? You know where?"

"Uh-huh."

Then Mitch put one arm across my dad's shoulders and led him away from us again. I could see Mitch grin and move his hands.

Leslie leaned toward me. "This'll be a cool summer, okay?" Her eyes were bright. She licked her lips.

Leslie was so squirmy and kind of smug that I asked, "What's up?"

"Nothing. I'll tell you tomorrow."

"Don't you have time to tell me nothing now? I mean, how long could it take?"

She glanced at her father. "Tomorrow, " she whispered. "It's a secret."

"Graham?" called my dad, walking toward us. "Is Beaufort okay?"

"Uh-huh. All his feed's gone, and he's lying down."

Leslie waved as she and Mitch turned away.

"I'll just check on him," Dad said.

"You're gonna check on him, too?" I asked.

He turned, frowning. He was wearing a baseball cap with RANCHMASTER FEED written on it, and he fiddled with the green bill for a second or two. "Well, son, I just meant that —"

"If you were going to check on him yourself anyway, why did you make me do it?"

He took his cap off and slapped it against one leg like it was dusty. "I didn't *make* you, I *asked* you —"

"And after you do ask me, and I tell you, why don't you believe me?"

My father studied the back of one hand. "What's the matter with you, Graham? You never used to be like this."

"Me? Dad, you don't even trust me to look at a horse and see if he's lying down or standing up."

Dad took a halter off the wall and inspected it for worn places. And kept inspecting it. Finally he stormed off.

"Great!" I yelled. "Another perfect conversation."

≡ ≡ ≡

Half an hour later, with my bike in the back of the Astro van, Dad took the long way home along the coast. We didn't talk at all for a while. Finally he said, "I'm sorry about that business with Beaufort."

"I'm sorry, too, I guess. Maybe I shouldn't have . . ."

"It wasn't that I didn't trust you. It's just . . . well, I'd like to win a lot of races this summer, and I want everything just so."

"I said it's okay. Really. And I should have been on time. I just got talking to Leslie . . ."

"Leslie's growin' up." His eyebrows arched. "Did you see those jeans? Mitch is kind of worried about her."

"Why?"

He took his eyes off the road for a second. "Seems like she ran around a lot when they were up north."

"Ran around?"

"Nothin' out of line, but not what he was used to."

"Is that what you guys were talking about when we came back from seeing Pepperoni?"

"Nope. This time Mitch was telling dirty jokes. He felt obliged to entertain me because he was borrowing money."

After a minute I asked, "Why don't Mitch's clients stay with him?"

"Son, he doesn't win enough races."

"He always gets new owners."

"Mitch *looks* right. Fifteen years ago when we were just starting out, he looked like a Marlboro ad. He still does."

That was true: Stetson hat, western shirt with pearl snaps, pressed jeans flared just right for boots made out of alligator, lizard, elephant, or ostrich. Tons of brown hair just starting to go gray where it showed under his hat brim, crinkly lines around his eyes like he'd been staring out across sunbaked prairies his whole life.

"Dad, tell me one of those jokes Mitch told you."

Dad tugged at the seat belt that sloped across his chest. "Nah."

"C'mon. I'm old enough."

"They aren't even funny."

"You were laughing."

"I was just being polite. He didn't win squat up north, so I figured he didn't need his jokes to lose, too."

Off to our right was a run-down trailer court. Outside one of those old aluminum jobs sat some guy with long blond hair firing up a bong.

"So tell me one, and *I'll* be polite."

"You won't like it. You probably won't get it."

"Try me."

He rattled it off: "A white horse fell in the mud." His eyes left the road for a second and landed on me. "There's your dirty joke."

"Dad, I heard that when I was six."

"Yeah? Well, check with me when you're twenty. In the meantime, you're not missin' much. Mitch's jokes are pretty stupid."

"Maybe I could decide that for myself." I spit the sentence out like it tasted bad.

Dad checked the rearview mirror, then let the car coast a dozen yards or so. "Do you feel okay, Graham?"

"I'm all right."

He shook his head. "If you were a horse, I'd have you scoped and wormed."

"I'm not sick, okay?"

A lot of the traffic had cleared, and I stared out toward the ocean, which looked still but wasn't. It was always moving, not really breathing, of course, but heaving up and down like breathing, like all the sleeping horses a few miles behind us. Like the people in the houses and apartments along this road. Like Dad and me.

We glided past the beat-up sign that said SCENIC VIEW, then stopped, and Dad switched off the ignition. There was only one other car a little way off.

He swung the door open. "Tide's out. Want to take a closer look?"

"I'm okay."

"Aw, c'mon."

"Dad," — suddenly I was talking through clenched teeth again — "if you want me to get out, say so. If you just want to know if I *want* to get out, believe me when I tell you, okay?"

He flicked a switch, and the tiltable steering wheel slammed up. "All right. I want you to get out. How's that?"

I swung my door so hard it bounced back at me. "Fine."

Toward the edge of the bluff, he hooked his thumbs in his jeans. I crossed both arms across my chest. If he'd had a holster and if I'd had some war paint on, we could have posed for a picture called *Cowboy and Indian*.

We stood there a long time, stiff and quiet. Finally he pointed toward the low wall of surf. "Could you ride those little waves?" he asked.

I shook my head and muttered, "Not enough to work with."

He nodded, then frowned. "How's your new board?"

"The one you bought me, right?"

"I didn't say that."

"Well, it's fine."

He shifted his weight, reached down, and rubbed his right leg where a horse had bit him. "When you left Pepperoni, did it look like she was going to rest?"

"Uh-huh."

"I don't know what to do about her. When she doesn't rest, I worry. When she does, she grows another inch."

"She's done growing."

"Uh-huh. That's what DiFiero says. He wants her to run tomorrow and says he'll ride her himself if he has to."

Dad grinned to himself. Maybe he was imagining his richest owner in a little jockey's outfit: those gaudy silks, that little bow tie.

I took half a step closer. "When'll she run, do you think?"

"Pretty much when I say so."

"Yeah, but when?"

Dad ran his tongue deep inside his lower lip and made a bulge. He did this when he was thinking. Or getting mad.

"I've been training for more years than you are old, Graham."

Oh, God, I thought, *not this again*.

"I may not be good at a lot of things, but I've got a feel for horses. And my feeling about this one is she's not as grown up as she looks, so she's not gonna run at Mariposa."

I leaned to spit.

Dad turned to me. "You think I'm wrong?"

"It doesn't matter what I think."

"Tell me."

"Why? You wouldn't listen anyway. Your feelings are the only ones that count."

"I can't believe you want to see her pulled up in front of the grandstand while the meat wagon comes for her."

"That's the last thing I want."

"'Cause it'd be my fault, not yours."

"It wouldn't happen."

"It happens all the time, and you know it." He pointed west. "You weren't raised out there like a fish. You were raised around a racetrack."

"Like a horse?"

"You got the best. There was nothin' that was too good for you."

"Oh, bull."

A little way off, somebody turned the radio on in the other car. Then the door opened, and a guy climbed out. He lit a cigarette and looked out over the shiny top.

Dad moved closer. He didn't whisper. He hissed at me. "I didn't get you out here to argue about Pepperoni or bore you with stories about how long I've been training. Mostly I just want to know what's wrong. You're not doin' drugs, are you?"

"Dad, Mom won't let me eat a candy bar. What are the chances I'm a heroin addict?"

"So, what's up?"

"With what?"

"With you."

"I'm fine."

He quoted me, "'Oh, bull.' You're moody. You're hard to get along with. You're as liable to argue as not." I could almost feel his eyes roaming over me. "So, what is it?"

Finally I said, "I don't know."

"You gotta know," he said. "Otherwise it goes on like this, and I don't want that."

"I'm a little confused, okay? So can there be a week or maybe even a month where things aren't just the way you want?"

"So you'll be all right by the first part of July?"

I couldn't believe it. "I didn't mean a month literally. I just meant time. Couldn't some time go by?"

He frowned and patted the top pocket of his checkered shirt. "This is enough to make me start smoking again, you know that?"

"Chew some gum," I said automatically.

"Your mother says this is just because you're almost fourteen. She says it's your glands talking or your hormones or something."

"Mom doesn't know everything."

"She also said you got a C in math."

I looked up at him. Right at him. "So?"

"Why?"

I took a big breath and let it out. "I think I was bored."

His mouth dropped. He looked like I'd slapped him with a fish. "My God, who's not bored?"

"You're not."

"Everybody is sometimes. I just don't screw up when I am."

"A C's not bad."

"It's not good."

"It's average."

"Would you want that on your tombstone: 'average'?"

"What difference does it make to you what grades I make? They're my grades. Why won't you just leave me alone?"

"I'm your father!" he shouted. "I can't leave you alone. I couldn't even if I wanted to."

We stood there and glared at each other until he broke off and stalked away along the edge of the bluff. And that's when I thought it: What if he slipped? Or what if there was a little earthquake? He'd just be gone, wouldn't he? And I'd never have to go through any of this stuff with him again.

≡ ≡ ≡

About eleven or so the next day, I was sitting on my board. That's pretty late, but I wasn't good enough yet to join the Dawn Patrol. That's what the early morning surfers were called, big guys who'd been at it for years and years and got up early to catch the best waves right off the pier.

I was half-full of salt water from catching an edge and getting thrashed one time too many, so I was shaking my head like an Irish setter and digging in my stopped-up ears when I saw Leslie watching me. She signaled as if I was the captain of a steamer and she was all by herself on No Place Atoll.

I wanted to ride in to her if I could, maybe get almost all the way to the beach and just step off nearly dry like it was nothing.

I turned around, lay out, and paddled hard. Then I sat up and eyeballed the set coming in. It wasn't much, but I liked being able to read it. Standing on the sand, all waves look pretty much alike to most people, the way litters of puppies can. I wasn't as good as lots of guys who surfed, but I knew better than that. In every litter there's a tough little guy, an extra playful one, a beauty, and a runt.

Well, I missed the beauty by ten yards, ducking my head and spearing through it, so I tried the playful one and stayed up maybe six seconds. But trying to pretend I could care less that Leslie was watching turned out to be too much pressure. The board just shot out from under me. I came down on my back — hearing the slap seemed to make it hurt more — and salt water shot up my nose.

I scrambled to my feet, teeth clenched, and waved one of those super-casual waves that meant, *I'm fine. No problem. Put me back in, Coach. Sure my arms are broken, but I'll carry the ball in my teeth.*

Leslie stood up. "Are you okay?"

Coughing, I reeled in my board and slogged toward

her. "I did that on purpose. Anybody can ride in like King Neptune."

"Uh-huh. Are you sure you're all right?"

I pulled my trunks up and shook some sand out of one leg. "Absolutely. I've almost got that perfected."

"Falling off?"

"I'm supposed to go all the way around, see," — I drew a circle in the air — "then land on my feet again. You can take a trick like that on the pro tour." Just then about a gallon of water ran out of my nose, and Leslie made a face. I hacked again. "Maybe I'll leave that part out."

"Want to sit down?"

I leaned over, both hands on my knees. "Just let me catch my breath."

"You're sure you're okay?"

"Are you kidding? I'm fine."

Right by my little pile of stuff, Leslie had laid out sunblock, a lime-green visor, some lotion, a couple of Cokes, and a Walkman.

"Catch," she said flapping out a long towel. I fought the offshore breeze getting it down, then anchored my end with my old Pumas. The towel was huge and brand new. It showed a couple in jeans and not much else and said GUESS? at the bottom.

It looked like a painting, so I sat down next to it in my wet, sandy trunks and watched Leslie shrug out of her drawstring pants and shirt, then stand there in a new green one-piece bathing suit with turquoise racing stripes.

She grinned down at me and ran a line of lotion the color of Cheez Whiz onto one leg. One long leg. When she started to rub it in, I had to look away. I was breathing hard, but not from surfing. Not anymore.

"I was watching you out there," she said, sitting down and threading her ponytail through the back of her visor. "You looked pretty good."

"I got inside the curl once. There's water all around you, but you're not really wet. It's such a great feeling."

"I've seen you. It looks cool."

"I could teach you," I said, getting up on my knees and brushing sand off. "You could use my old board."

"Nah." She fiddled with her rose-colored Vuarnet sunglasses. "I could never do that." She flipped onto her stomach and, without looking, held out the squeeze bottle of suntan lotion. "Do the backs of my knees, okay? I don't want to burn."

Her skin was so white I could see a tiny blue vein. I knew it meandered through her whole body until it reached her heart and started around again. My blood, on the other hand, had all rushed into my swimming trunks, which started to stir. I flipped the towel over them, like I was cold.

"Graham?"

"Right. I'm here. I'm getting my hands warm first."

I squirted the stuff on and rubbed. I pretended I was waxing my board. I pretended I was sanding something or petting a dolphin. Anything to avoid thinking about how soft her skin was.

I finished just before I had to rush into the ocean, raise the temperature of the water, and upset the entire balance of nature. Then I dropped beside her, face down. When I plowed into the sand, I gave this pitiful little moan.

Leslie looked up. "What was that?"

I glanced around. "What was what?"

"That sound."

I shrugged and looked west. "A seal?"

She looked at me like I was nuts, then held out half a headset.

"When did you get a Walkman?" I asked, glad to be talking about something.

"Up north." She shook the Walkman and frowned. "It was like you had to have one." She moved her head back and forth, doing a little stationary boogie. "Everybody's rocking out between classes and at lunch." A shrug. "So I get this thing, but then I can never find any music, just people talking about UFOs and God and recipes for cheese balls."

"Maybe it's not a Walkman. Maybe it's a Talkman."

An indulgent smirk. She started to draw in the sand, making a big *L*, then a big *T*. Then she drew a circle around the letters, like a brand for cattle.

"What was it like up there, anyway?" I asked.

"San Francisco?" She scrunched up her face. "There were just these girls with fake nails and push-up bras and stuff, and you were either their friend or else you were totally out of it."

"So were you friends with them?"

Down came her glasses so she could glare at me over the neon-green top.

"Well, not exactly. One day we're by the lockers just outside the cafeteria, okay? And they're standing around with their little ninety-dollar purses, right? But they condescend to ask me what my dad does. So I say he's a trainer. So they say, 'Oh, for the Olympics?' 'No,' I say, 'for thoroughbreds.' So then they look at each other, and one goes, 'Like their personal trainer?'" Leslie fell backward in disgust.

"They thought Mitch went from stall to stall with an aerobics tape and some free weights?"

Leslie started to giggle. "And I start to picture those ten tired old horses we had up there dressed in spandex pants and sweatbands, and the next thing I know I'm laughing in their faces."

"Which did not make them ask you to their big white houses in the pines."

"Right." She rolled onto her stomach again, propped up on her elbows, and stared straight ahead. She looked a little like the Sphinx. But not so hard to figure out. "It all just made me want to call you and talk about horses. It made me want my dad to lose so he'd get discouraged and come on back down south." She turned to look at me. "Isn't that a great thing for a daughter to wish on her father?"

I remembered being on the bluff last night. "There are worse thoughts than that," I muttered.

"Anyway," she said, tugging at the top of her suit, "most of the time I didn't like it up there. And when I did like it, I couldn't tell anybody."

"Who's anybody?"

"You know — Dad."

"Why not?"

"Are you kidding? He would've gone nuts."

"About what? That you weren't popular? What would Mitch care if you were —"

Suddenly she scrambled up, reached for the Cokes, opened them both, and gave me one. "Tell me about you," she said, plopping down beside me. "How was school? How'd you do at Santa Anita?"

I looked at her, but she wouldn't look back. She rolled the Coke can between her hands, then picked at a hard place on one foot. So finally I said, "Santa Anita was okay, I guess. We won . . . I mean Mom and Dad won the San Jacinto Stakes with Balkan Serenade."

"Good for them," she said, trying to mean it, but her heart wasn't in it. She kept frowning and drawing in the sand.

"Do you really want to know about school?" I asked.

She smoothed out the place where she'd been scrawling *L* and *T*.

"Sure."

"Well, remember Seymour Hermann?"

She sat up straighter. "That kid who never said two words? Sat in the back of our homeroom?"

"Yeah. He shaved half his head and bought a leather jacket so he'd look cool."

"It's hard to picture Seymour being cool."

"He doesn't want to be called Seymour, either. He changed his name to Vermin."

"Vermin Hermann?"

"Even Mrs. Caliverri calls him Vermin. He won't answer her unless she does. One time in history we're talking about the Middle Ages, and she wants to know about how the Black Plague was spread so she calls on him: 'Vermin?' And since that's the answer, we all say, 'That's right.' And everybody but him laughs.

"Even Mrs. Caliverri?"

"Especially Mrs. Caliverri."

Leslie took a long swallow of Coke and wiped her mouth with the back of one hand; so I did, too. Then we just sat and watched the ocean for a while.

"I am really glad to be back in Mariposa," she said all of a sudden. "I understand things better when I'm here." She looked at me kind of defiantly. "Don't you, Graham?"

"Sometimes."

I stared down at my knees while I thought about how I used to love Mariposa, too, how it used to be the perfect place. But this year was different. And since *it* hadn't changed, that left me.

All of a sudden the wind died down, and I could feel how hot my skin was; I wiggled into my shorts and my red zip-up sweatshirt.

"Don't burn," I said to Leslie, who'd lain back and closed her eyes. "It's your first day."

"Hmm." She stretched and spread her legs, making a big X.

I made myself think about the sandpipers, the ocean, the ships outlined on the horizon like the ones I used to draw when I was little.

Another couple of surfers were walking our way, a blond guy and his buddy, who had black hair, wet-looking and shiny as shoe polish. The blond — with the standard zinced nose and nonstandard trunks with sharks on them — had a big old stoker board, way too long and heavy for his size. They were laughing about who-knows-what, but when they got closer — fifteen yards away, maybe — one of them stopped, nudged his buddy, and they looked at us. At Leslie. Tilting their heads to get just the right angle. Complete sleazoids.

I was on my feet just like that, jogging toward them over the hot sand.

"All right, guys," I said. "Nothin' to see here. Move along now."

"Gee, officer. We just wanted to give the babe in the green suit some mouth-to-mouth."

"Fine. Very funny." I shuffled a little closer, waving

my hands like I was herding geese. "This way out, okay?"

The dark guy looked down. "Now look what you've done. You got sand on my foot."

"Yeah, well, that happens on the beach."

The other one peered around me toward Leslie. "What's your name, sweet stuff?"

I stepped in front of him. "She hasn't got a name, okay. She's an alien."

"I hate it when somebody kicks sand on my feet."

"Take him out," advised Mr. Sharks-on-His-Trunks.

Gulp. "Then you'll get blood on your hands," I said, retreating. "You don't want that, do you? Sand on your feet. Blood on your hands. Next you'll get —"

That's when he pushed me, and since I was backpedaling anyway, down I went, landing on my tailbone with a thump.

He pointed his finger at me like a vice-principal. "Stay there unless you want some more, you little mall rat."

I tried to look natural. Like I'd wanted to sit down. Except that I was breathing fast and shallow. I knew I was in trouble. Very few fights are won from a seated position.

Then they wandered off, laughing and shaking their heads and exchanging about a thousand cult handshakes to celebrate their great triumph. I scrambled back to the towel.

"What was that all about?" asked Leslie.

I brushed sand off my behind. My hands were shaking a little. "If those guys were thinking what I think they were thinking, I didn't want them thinking it about you."

"The blond one was cute."

"Oh, great. I risk a life-threatening injury and —"

"You only fell on your butt."

"So? So? Try to do anything without your butt."

"How do you know what they were thinking?"

I looked down at the sand. "Because I think those things sometimes."

She took a sip of Coke. "About me?"

"No! I mean, no. Not when I can help . . . Just no, okay?

I watched Leslie pull on her long pants and tie the drawstring.

"Anyway, I didn't know if you saw 'em," I said. "I thought you were asleep."

"I didn't exactly see them, but I knew they were look-ing." She glanced at me, then away. "Donna's told me about, you know, keeping my legs crossed and stuff." She rolled her eyes, finished her Coke, and shook the can. "Bein' fourteen is more of a problem than I thought it was going to be."

"Being almost fourteen is no piece of cake, either, okay?"

I could see her squint behind her sunglasses. "What are you mad at?"

"Nothing. Jeez. I'm not mad, okay?"

Leslie looked toward the road that led past Mariposa

Downs. She tugged at her suit. "Anyway, speaking of problems?"

"Yeah?"

She started to put things into her blue bag with the thick white zipper. "This is what I couldn't tell you last night, what I didn't want Dad to know."

The couple painted on her new towel were kissing, and Leslie outlined the boy's long arm as it wound around. "The thing is, I've got a boyfriend."

A boyfriend. Leslie's got a boyfriend. The last time I'd heard that was in something like second grade. A bunch of girls were chanting that snotty schoolyard thing: "Leslie's got a boyfriend. Leslie's got a boyfriend." I even remembered the kid's name — Marty Kreplowski.

"You mean like dates and stuff?" I asked.

"Uh-huh. That's the only part that made me want to stay in San Francisco."

"What kind of dates?"

She hugged her knees. "Just the regular kind, like you go places and then later on you're alone." She let her hands fall open. "You know."

"How would I know?"

"I guess I meant 'understand.'"

I started to brush away every grain of sand on my feet. Then finally I asked, "So who is he then? Somebody from the track up there?"

When she slipped her glasses off and let them dangle from the red braided cord, her eyes were the brightest

I'd ever seen, but not like the sun was reflecting off them; it was more like they were lit from inside.

"Graham, he is so cool! He's a classical guitarist, and he looks like one of those Greeks we learned about in school."

"He wears a toga?"

"Don't be dumb. I meant like a Greek god."

"Leslie, Greeks played lutes, or pipes or something. Not guitars."

"I just meant how cute he is and how he's, you know, talented, and sensitive and vulnerable and all those things boys are supposed to be."

"According to who?"

"Well, you know, talk shows and *Seventeen* and things like —"

"Oh, well. That settles it, especially if it's in *Seventeen*."

I pretended to adjust my hat while I snuck a glance at myself in her sunglasses. I looked all right, I suppose, but not exactly cute. I was about as sensitive as a horseshoe lately. And as far as talent goes, I could wrap Kleenex around a comb and play "She'll Be Comin' Round the Mountain When She Comes."

"Want to know his name?" Leslie asked, beaming.

For her sake I said, "Sure."

"Webster. Isn't it a great name?"

"From the same people who brought us the dictionary?"

"And his first name is even cooler." She closed her eyes and uttered the single word: "Todd." When she'd recovered from the effect of those four magic letters, she said, "He sang in assembly once." She scooted closer and wrapped her hand around my wrist. "It was so cool. He had his hair pulled back real tight and tied with a little piece of velvet that matched his jacket. And the whole time he stared down right at me."

I pried at her fingers. "Just stop cutting off the circulation, okay? I might need this hand for something someday."

She glanced around and leaned closer. I could smell the cocoa butter in her lotion. "Guess what he did one night."

I tried to shake some feeling back into my hand. "Fell off the stage and died?"

"He and some other guys came over and TP'ed my house!" Then she rolled back and clenched both fists as if she'd just made a great save in volleyball. "He likes me, Graham. He really likes me."

I shot to my feet. "Big deal," I snapped. "So Romeo TP'd the Capulet house. So what?"

The light in Leslie's eyes had gone out. Her mouth was partly open.

"I thought," she finally whispered, "that you'd be glad for me."

I put my hands over my eyes. Not peekaboo style, but with the heels of them shutting out the light. I sat that way for probably an entire minute. Then I murmured, "Your problem is that you've got a boyfriend, right?"

"Todd's not the problem," she answered with an edge. "Dad's the problem."

I took my hands away, blinked, and hunkered down next to her. Naturally she retreated. "Well, I've got a problem, too. Slowly but surely I'm turning into a complete butt-face."

"You're telling me." But she leaned toward me again. A big fly with greenish wings landed on my arm, and she reached to shoo it away. Then she asked, "What's goin' on?"

"For a couple of months now I've been about half-mad all the time."

"At what?

I shook my head. "I wish I knew."

When she twisted to look over her shoulder, I did, too. Cars were starting to fill up the coast road. Racetrack traffic. People going in to play the daily double or to just get the best of the free seats.

"Your dad's got a horse in the second race," she said. "We'd better go." All very snipped off and prim.

"Look, I'm sorry about before. What I said, I mean. And how I said it."

It was her turn to stand up and look down at me. Then she tugged at the towel, so I rolled away as she folded it up herself.

Finally she said, "I know a lot about horses, but I don't know anything about boys." She shifted the towel and the blue bag from one hand to the other. "I think I need some lessons."

"Not from me, Leslie."

"But we're best friends. I always ask you, Graham."

"And I always tell you to go to the library and look it up."

"This stuff isn't in the library. Where am I gonna look up how to act around Todd or what to think when he says I'm pretty?" She squinted at me through her sunglasses. "Do boys always say things like that?"

I shook my head. "I don't know."

"Do *you*?"

"Why would I? I don't have a girlfriend, remember?"

"I meant do you think I'm pretty."

"Jeez, Leslie. Sure."

She bit her lip. Concentrating. Then a car horn made us both look toward the traffic and the track, so we trudged toward the strand, not saying anything. If I drifted toward her, she drifted away. Then just before we hit the sidewalk, back she came. I shifted my board to the other side, just to be that little bit closer.

Where the sidewalk started, we stopped and kicked sand out of our flip-flops. Sitting in rows on the hot concrete were a bunch of newspaper vending machines. Some were legit, like for the *L.A. Times*, the *Mariposa Bugle*, and the *Recycler*. But there was one called *Sun & Fun: A Nudist Journal*.

We stared at the cover.

"Could you be undressed like that?" she asked. "Even with somebody you liked?"

"Not without a bigger volleyball."

Leslie laughed so loud that people on the street looked at her. I grinned, too. Not because I was so funny but because I liked making Leslie laugh. And because I knew she wasn't mad anymore.

She held one palm up. I slapped it hard. She grabbed and held on.

"Why do I like you so much, Graham?"

"I don't know, but don't stop."

≡　≡　≡

Around one-thirty, I locked my bike to the water trough by Dad's office, then, as always, checked on Pepperoni. She put her head out of the stall so I could rub her nose. I liked to look into her huge eyes, down past the flecked brown part to the gold center. It seemed — I don't know — completely quiet down there. Serene.

Then she raised her head, whooshed at my hair, and slobbered on me. Which just made me smile and rub her harder. I didn't think Pepperoni loved me, exactly. I wasn't sure animals could do that. Or if they could, I wasn't sure it was anything like human love. But I knew she liked and trusted me. And for her to keep liking and trusting me I only had to show up at the barn and not be mean to her. That's all. There was nothing else I had to do, nobody else I had to be. No grade I had to make. No word I had to say or not say.

I reached for the halter and put my forehead against her big, wet nose. "You're the best horse in the world," I whispered. "Not just the biggest, but the best. And there's nothing that you can't do, okay? Absolutely nothing."

Just then I heard somebody coming, so I made a big deal out of inspecting the filly's teeth.

"Doesn't matter to me if you talk to horses," Leslie said with a grin. "Just tell me first if she ever answers so I can get us on *That's Incredible*."

"Hold her, will you? I want to take a look at something."

I'd barely hunkered down, when Leslie slipped in and latched the door behind her. "Graham," she said slowly, "what do you think about most of the time?"

I was busy with Pepperoni, running both hands down her smooth side, then putting my ear there and listening to her breathe. "Umm, I don't know. Lots of things. Ever since last night, I've been trying to figure out if I think the thoughts up myself or if they come in from outside." I glanced Leslie's way as Pepperoni let me feel around on one of her hooves. "I mean, am I like a guy in a workshop who makes stuff, or am I like a clerk in a crummy hotel who lets almost anybody in?"

"So boys think about being hotel clerks?"

I banged my head lightly on Pepperoni's knee. "No, and remind me to keep my deepest thoughts to myself from now on."

"C'mon. Please? I need to know what boys think about."

I slumped back against the nearest wall, "All right. All right. Cars, girls, and french fries."

"Cars first?"

"It's like all one word — carsgirlsandfrenchfries."

"Todd's going to get a car in sixty-two days."

I stood up. "I'm so happy for him."

"And he's got a girl."

"So all he needs is a potato."

"Is this going to always make you mad?" she asked, ducking under Pepperoni's head as we changed sides. Then before I could answer she added, "Take hold of that left front. Does it feel a little warm to you?"

I frowned and felt Pepperoni's ankle. "She's fine. You're probably just hot all over from thinking about Mr. Sensitive."

Just then we heard the first faint notes of "Boots and Saddle," that little trumpet solo everybody thinks of as the call to the post. So we said good-bye to Pepperoni and headed out of the backstretch.

I have to admit, I liked buying a program and walking in with the fans. I liked seeing the track again. In Arcadia, where we lived most of the year, smog dulled things, filed the edges off the San Gabriel Mountains, the buildings, even the leaves on the big tulip tree in our backyard.

But at Mariposa, the sea breezes gave everything

permission to be itself: yellows were buttery, reds were hot and fiery, oranges citrusy. And my geometry teacher would have loved how the red tile roofs met the white-washed walls and all the clean lines everything had.

Waiting at the foot of the escalator, I opened my program to the second race. We were running . . . I mean Dad was running Winter Syntax. Under *Trainer* it said John Carpenter and under *Owner,* Warren DiFiero.

As I stepped onto the escalator, I thought about *owner, trainer, Dad.* And then *son, teenager, confused.* Most people were funny about words. They treated them like hard-boiled eggs — nothing to be careful with and plenty more where those came from. I wasn't so sure. Leslie would never admit it, but she was thinking about words, too. Todd's words, anyway. And whether he meant what he said.

We slid off the escalator together, then drifted toward the good seats. My dad had bought the same ones right on the finish line for as long as I could remember, and Mitch had his back a little and off to the left.

Everybody around us knew each other. A dozen people said hello to me, said how I'd grown or — just kidding around — reached for my baseball hat, the one with SURFSIDE on it.

It's funny, when I wasn't actually at the races, it was easy to think that I might not want to follow in my Dad's footsteps. That was an idea that had started to tick me off, anyway. Why should I tiptoe around after him? My future wasn't a murky swamp that only he knew the way through. But then I actually went to the track, and — sure enough — I loved it. Just like he did.

I said hi to Dave, the usher who more or less guarded the seats, then spotted Mom sitting by herself with a book, as usual.

When she looked up, I waved and she motioned for me. I glanced at Leslie, already bent over a racing form with her dad and two other guys. As if she could feel me looking at her, her eyes swept up from the paper and landed on me, then swept down again.

I slipped in beside my mother and felt her arm go around me. Part of me wanted to lean into her the way I used to — just close my eyes and feel her heart beat, smell the Estée Lauder I'd bought for her birthday. Another part wanted to slump and stare at the ground. It didn't want her arm around me at all.

"Did you eat the sandwich I left you at home?"

"Mom, I'm not so dumb I won't eat when I'm hungry."

"Nobody said you were dumb. And don't sit like that; you'll turn into a hunchback."

Just then Mitch came up behind us and sat down. He put one hand on my mom's shoulder, and she leaned back without turning around and looked at him upside down, like an acrobat.

"Hey, Mitch."

"Susan." Then he offered me his extremely hard and calloused hand. Racetrack people shake hands *a lot*.

"Anybody to bet in here?"

Mom said, "John's got his eye on something for Warren." She glanced down at her program. "The seven horse, Legal Eagle. But when they walked by, he looked fat to me."

Mitch got up and glanced at the big neon board where the horses' odds were flashing.

"Thanks," he said, drifting away.

I could see my father down the way talking to Warren DiFiero and his friends. Behind me, Mitch had slid up alongside another man, and they were trading secrets like kids passing notes. Leslie, carrying a giant Coke, slipped past Dave, and when he said something to her, they both looked at the horses way across on the backstretch. Two men and a woman hurried past me and I heard ". . . ran good at Ascot, and we can get her for two and a half if we do it now."

The box seats were everybody's office. Sure, it was fun and people had a good time, but in the last couple of years I'd seen just how much business got done, too. Buying and selling, trading and gossiping, wheeling and dealing.

But nobody lied, and nobody went back on his word. If a person said he wanted in and then shook on it, that was that. We were in California and it was the nineties, but it was the Old West, too. You gave your word, and you meant it.

Just before post time, Dad came back and sat with us. He put his hand around my neck and pretended he was going to twist my head around like an owl's. But when

I stiffened up and it looked as if he might break a few vertebrae, he let go, raised his binoculars, and watched the horses.

When the race went off, I turned around, my back to the track. I liked to see all those different people in the stands in their Hawaiian shirts and shorts and sundresses and bolo ties and flowered hats turn into one thing — the crowd, like individual grains of Jell-O turning into dessert.

As the horses angled for home, they— or it — started to roar. I leaned back a little when the sound hit me, then glanced at Leslie, who had both fists clenched, at her dad, teeth gritted so hard his jaw quivered, and at Mr. DiFiero and his fancy friends hopping up and down.

Then the horses poured under the wire, and it was over. The cheering died like somebody running out of breath, and the crowd broke up again into twenty-four thousand little pieces.

Dad sat down. "That seven's got a nice way of going," he said. "Warren might be right about him."

"John! John!"

We all turned to see Mr. DiFiero waving, his pinky ring glittering.

"Now, why," Dad asked nobody in particular, "doesn't he just walk over here if he wants something?"

"I just did the books. We could get along without him," Mom said, "if we had to."

Dad let out a chestful of air. "I don't want to just get

along, though." Then he dug into his pocket. "Get us Cokes, will you, Graham?"

"I don't want a Coke."

"Well, will you get your mom and me one?"

"I got them last time."

Mom put her book down. "Graham, what'd I tell you yesterday about being crabby?"

A minute later I stood in line and listened to the horseplayers. "They let that last long shot come in to drive us crazy," said the guy behind me to everybody and nobody.

They. Forces beyond his control who manipulated every race. I may have been a thirteen-year-old indentured servant, but even I knew better than that. Anything could happen in a horse race.

I plopped down beside Mom, put Dad's Coke on an empty seat, and handed her a big red and white cup.

Just below us, down on the bricks where people brought their beach chairs and coolers and made a day of it, I spotted a couple of guys I'd seen in the surfing magazines.

They were tanned like crazy all over, and they looked strong. Both of them had blond hair bleached out almost white and pulled back in little ponytails. I tried to picture myself in one of those. Talking to my dad.

"See those guys?" I pointed them out to Mom.

"Remind me," she said, "to buy a tub of Oil of Olay and just sit in it. Lord, what's happened to their skin?"

"They're professional surfers."

"Either that or big pieces of beef jerky."

"I might like to do that," I said.

She was reading the inside cover of a paperback. "Do what, honey?"

"Surf."

"You already do."

I glanced at her out of the corner of my eyes. "I mean when I grow up." When I couldn't stand the silence, I added, "Some guys do, you know."

"Grow up?"

"Surf professionally. There's a tour and everything. You travel all over the world and just surf."

"Sounds like fun."

"What do you think Dad would do?"

"He probably wouldn't go unless they had sea horse races."

I refused to laugh or even smile. "Do you think he'd be mad because I might want to do something besides train thoroughbreds?"

"Just because he trains doesn't mean that you have to, does it?"

"I guess part of me thinks it does."

She turned in her seat. "Is that what all of this is about, Graham?"

"All of what?"

"You know — the way you've been lately. You're not worried about your future, are you?"

"I don't know. Not exactly. A little, maybe."

"Honey, you're thirteen."

I stood up. "Almost fourteen. And so what? Lots of kids worry. You know Kenny Heyden, our second baseman? He's got an ulcer!"

"But, Graham . . ."

Just then a blond woman sat down on the other side of Mom and started to talk. I saw a paperback come out of her purse. My mother liked to read, and all summer she and some of the other wives traded books.

Lots of them were the thick kind with a couple on the cover: he was a pirate, and she was a lady in a low-cut dress. Or he was a Yankee soldier, and she was a Southern belle in a low-cut dress. If he'd been a stallion, she'd have been a mare. In a low-cut dress.

But Mom read hard stuff, too. There were books all over the condominium already, lying half-open, spines up, like tents scattered around a campground.

I felt a cool hand on the back of my neck. "Hey," said Leslie. "Want to go for a walk or something?"

Mom took hold of my arm. "Sweetheart," she whispered, "this is a vacation. Worry in September, okay?"

"Sure."

She reached for her purse. "Need some money?"

I said, "No."

Leslie said, "Yes," but she was grinning.

As we rode down the escalator, I asked, "What's up?"

"Why does anything have to be up? Why can't I just want to see my friend Graham?"

"Because you've got that look again."

"Relax, for heaven's sake. It's just an innocent little walk."

There was a tunnel that ran under the racetrack, connecting the grandstand to the infield. Years ago we'd discovered that if you were down there during a race you could hear the horses. Usually we'd be all alone, so we'd scream like we were being trampled and then run back out into the sun.

Leslie led the way through a maze of beach chairs and blankets to the slanty entrance. Inside, somebody'd had the bright idea to decorate the white walls. Naturally, they'd painted horses, and we slumped against a wild-eyed chestnut who would be second forever. Leslie was wearing jeans and a green tank top. She turned so the cool tunnel wall would be against her bare back.

"I'm just gonna write to Todd," she said abruptly, "and tell him to pick a weekend. His father's always flying to San Diego on business, and my dad's got to know sometime."

"Is that why you got me down here? I knew there was no such thing as an innocent little walk with you. Not these days, anyway."

Leslie slid closer. "How do you think I ought to start the letter: Dear Todd, Dearest Todd, Hi Todd, Yo Todd, Howdy Todd, Hey Todd, or what?"

"Definitely Dearest Todd. I keep picturing him in little velvet socks, eating a crumpet, whatever that is. Can we go now?"

"Wait. What about the ending? I don't want to say Love, Leslie. I might not love him. I might just be attracted to him."

"Then how about Magnetically Yours?"

Leslie laughed. She reached up and adjusted my cap. "You're cool, Graham."

"We're underground."

"You know what I mean."

That embarrassed me, so I did a few dozen standing push-ups against the cool concrete. A few people trudged by. Some had their picnic baskets and coolers closed up. They were done for the day, either sun-burned or broke, or both. One last couple ambled past. His arm was draped over her shoulder, fingers brushing the edge of her blue tube top.

"Do you think I'm flat?" Leslie asked abruptly.

"You mean like a cat that's been run over by a truck about a thousand times?"

Leslie gave me a look of pure pity. "Not all over," she said patiently. Then she looked down. "Just in places."

I shot across to the other side of the tunnel. And not entirely on purpose, either. I was just, well, propelled.

Leslie waited for some little kids to go pounding through; then she slid up next to me. "Could you like somebody who was, you know, flat upstairs?"

I turned around and put my burning forehead against the concrete.

"Leslie, please. This stuff embarrasses me."

"Tell me one thing, then, okay? One thing and I won't ask any more today." Then she took a giant step away and turned sideways. "Do *you* think I'm flat?"

"You're not flat, okay?"

"You didn't look!"

"I already looked. I looked before."

"When?"

"Never mind when. Just believe me — I looked."

"And?"

"I told you. You're not flat."

"I look flat to myself."

I turned around. "Why don't you ask Donna this stuff?"

"I do. And she laughs and says to be patient."

"Did you ask my mom?"

Leslie crossed her eyes, made a goofy face, and quoted, "'Be patient.'" Then she patted me on the shoulder. Pals. Buddies. "Thanks."

I pulled at my T-shirt. "Can we go now? I'm burning up down here."

At the entrance to the tunnel, I stopped in the bright sunlight and let the ocean breeze blow on me.

"Graham? When we really grow up, are we still going to have our barns side by side and help each other train like we said?"

I looked up. Above me the clouds made a galleon, a ghost, and a sheep. "What about Todd?"

"If he was still in the picture, he'd be on the road a

lot giving concerts. And anyway, by that time you'll have a girlfriend or a wife or something, too."

"With my luck, it'll be a something."

"Your wife'll be cute. Believe me."

I had my eyes closed, but I heard the soft rasp of Leslie's Levi's as she eased up beside me.

"Graham?" she whispered.

This time I could hear it coming. "The clinic is closed, Leslie. The doctor is out."

"When boys get excited — I mean after they've been parked with somebody or saying good night for about three hours — if they don't get, you know, relief, they don't die or anything, do they?"

I shaded my eyes. "Leslie, if guys who were frustrated died, you wouldn't be able to drive to the dry cleaners for all the bodies in the streets."

"But are you in pain or anything?"

"Not exactly. A little. Sometimes."

"When did this happen to you?"

"Right now. My head is killing me, thanks to you."

"I meant the other."

I sighed. "There was this birthday party a couple of months ago, okay, where they played these games, and I spent a lot of time in the closet with Maureen Selma."

"Kissing?"

"No, trying on culottes. Of course kissing."

"Did you moan on the way home?"

"I don't remember."

"Why do boys moan?"

"It's like a mating call. But if you aren't careful, moose come from miles around."

"Todd moans a lot."

I leaned over and brushed invisible grass off my khaki shorts. "I don't want to hear about it."

"Okay, but don't get mad."

I groped for my sunglasses, which were hanging around my neck. "I'm not mad."

She adjusted her green top. "I need to know this stuff. I've thought a lot about everything you've told me so far. And it helps."

I was looking at the ground, both hands stuck in my back pockets. Leslie bent down and peered up at me. "Okay?" She looked funny half upside down like that. And cute, too, with her hair swept over to one side. "Okay?" she repeated.

"Okay. Okay."

She straightened up. "Now. Let's go make some money. Dad's hot for a horse called Turtle Bridge."

There was one more race, the ninth, called the nightcap or the getaway race. It was a pretty desperate affair usually, with cheap horses running and anxious people betting, not even trying to win anymore, just get even.

Leslie went to find Mitch. I sat with Mom, remembering when I'd been so little my feet didn't touch the floor so I'd swung my legs all the time, pretending they were vines and Tarzan leaped from one to the other on his way through the jungle. But they weren't vines. They were legs. To stand up on.

Mom's hand smoothed my hair, then pointed: dusk was coming. The neon numbers pulsed; the grass on the turf course shimmered; the infield lake glowed.

"Pretty isn't it?" she said.

I just slid to the other side of the hard seat.

"What a pain in the butt," Dad said, plopping down heavily beside me.

Mom stretched one arm across me, and Dad touched his fingers to hers.

"DiFiero?" she asked.

"That's the one."

"What's he want?"

"Everything. And right now."

That made me sit up straight. "Are we talking about Pepperoni?"

He waited just a little too long. "Not exactly." Dad looked across me. "What's it called when somebody can't wait for something that takes time but he wants it anyway?"

"Immediate gratification," Mom murmured.

"That's right! Immediate gratification — that's him."

The announcer said, "Five minutes."

Dad glanced out across the track, then reached around and whipped out his racing form.

"Let's bet this race, Graham. Let's win a lot of money and go out to dinner." He opened the paper and leaned into it. Dad had taught me to read the fine print packed with more information than an encyclopedia: where the horse had raced last, when, who had ridden him, how well, where he'd finished, and why.

I didn't go as deep or as fast as my dad, but I liked doing it, following his finger from one horse's history to another, listening to him figure out loud. Or I used to like it.

"So," he asked, "it's Note Pad, right?"

"I don't know." I pointed. "What about Turtle Bridge?"

Dad frowned. "Are you kidding? That horse is sore. Everybody knows that."

I pointed. "He won last time."

"All the more reason to think he'll come apart today." Dad stood up. "Ten across on Note Pad, okay?"

Gulp. "No."

He stopped dead, half out of the box. I stood up, too, and took a deep breath. "I really think Turtle Bridge can win again."

"Damn it, Graham. That's just throwin' money away."

I had to swallow hard before I could say, "Look, Dad. You asked me who I liked, okay? And I told you."

"I know, son, but —"

"Why is it always 'but'? I don't think you really want to know who I like. You just want me to agree with you." I looked up at him. "Is that the deal — that you'll humor me until I come around to your way of thinking, and if I don't, you'll tell me I'm stupid?"

I was getting weak in the knees, but Dad was just

getting mad. "I never called you stupid. When did I ever call you stupid? I'm the one who taught you to handicap, that's all, so I hate to see you do it like a fool."

"Oh, great. A fool. Well, that's a real compliment. Thank God — excuse me, I know you don't want me to swear until I'm as wonderful at it as you are. So thank *gosh* you called me a fool instead of stupid."

"Look, Graham —"

But I was on a roll by then, holding onto the back of the green seat so my hands wouldn't shake. "And how do you know I'm a fool, anyway? The race isn't over yet. You're not God. You don't know everything. Why not at least wait and see before you call me names?"

"Whoa," Mom said, dropping an arm between us like one of those wooden things at a railroad crossing. "Acting as the referee for the Mariposa Boxing Commission, I hereby call this a draw."

Mom and I both glanced at Dad. He was staring off into space, the muscle in his jaw dancing.

"One minute," said the announcer.

"I don't need this," Dad muttered, and he stalked off toward the betting windows.

I heard somebody, almost for sure Leslie, come up behind me. I felt her hands on my shoulders. "Who do you want to bet?" she whispered.

I twisted around in the seat. "Turtle Bridge."

"Don't do it just because my dad likes him. He hasn't cashed a ticket all day."

"I can read a form," I snapped. "And Mitch is due. Anyway, I've got a pretty big hunch about this horse."

"All right. All right." She looked up at the board. "Just give me the money. I need to find somebody to bet for us."

I slipped her six dollars — all I had — and stood up. "And then let's go sit with *your* dad."

"Meet you there." And she was gone.

"Graham?" Mom tried to stop me as I swung out toward the aisle.

"I don't know what's wrong, okay?" I said. "And if I did, it might not be any of your business. So please just let me by."

The race was half-over before Leslie came back and handed me the folded ticket. "I almost got shut out."

"Maybe we'd be better off."

She took it all in and groaned. Note Pad was opening up with every stride while poor old Turtle Bridge was stuck down along the rail, going nowhere.

As the field swept under the wire and the winners crowed, I tore up my ticket in disgust. "What's the matter with me, anyway? How could I bet a racehorse named turtle anything?" I snatched my hat and wrung it like it'd been soaked. "What's my dad doing now? Probably giving away handfuls of money and telling people what a jerk I am."

"C'mon. He's not like that." She glanced toward my

parents' box. "He's just sitting there, talking to your mom."

Suddenly I was so tired. I fell back into the wooden seat and smoothed my hat out, then put it on. It was probably at a cocky angle, but I sure didn't feel cocky. "I know," I said. "But I just hate it that he's right all the time."

PART TWO

≡Mom and I spent the Fourth of July in Los Angeles visiting Grandma. And the first thing I wanted to do when I got back to the track was see Leslie.

An exercise rider in green leather chaps with shaggy fringe on them told me I'd just missed her, so I headed out of the backstretch cafeteria toward Mitch's barns, holding a folded napkin to my swollen lip.

"Graham!" She spotted me first and came running. Which made me grin. Which made me wince.

"What happened?" She stared at my face.

"I woke up early and couldn't go back to sleep, so I thought I'd try surfing with the Dawn Patrol."

She took the napkin away from me, folded it, and pressed. Hard. "Did you fall off and hit your head on your own board like you used to?"

"That happened once. Jeez, you make it sound like I did it every day." I tugged at her wrist. "Take it easy."

"It won't stop bleeding if I don't press hard."

"You're cutting off the blood to my entire head. Keep that up and my nose will fall off."

81

"Okay. Okay. What happened?"

"I got in some guy's way, and he just popped me."

"His way? There's not exactly double yellow lines out there."

I looked toward the ocean. "The waves were huge, and I got all turned around. There were boards everywhere and people yelling." I shrugged. "I got scared and paddled back in. But the next thing I know this big, hairy guy storms up and decks me. He told me to grow the hell up before I tried that again."

"When I saw you, I thought maybe you and your dad got into it."

I shook my head. "Dad never even spanked me when I was little. You know that." Leslie took the napkin away, stepped back, and checked me out.

"I think it's stopped. Just don't go kissing Maureen Selma in any closets for a while."

"That happened one time."

"And where were you for the whole Fourth of July weekend?"

"At Grandma's house."

"Which is in Los Angeles."

"But not next door to Maureen Selma and her closet."

Leslie wadded up the slightly bloody napkin and made a nice shot into the nearest trash can.

"Did you watch the reruns?

She meant films of the races that the sports channel showed every night.

"Uh-huh. We saw Dad win the feature."

"And my dad lose the one just before that."

I tried to sound optimistic. "There's lots of races."

"Sure."

Leslie kicked at one of the sparrows that always hung around the barns, missing it by a mile. She was wearing her old rough-out boots, some washed-out jeans, and a checkered shirt with a stiff place on the back where she'd mended a tear with some of that iron-on stuff.

"I tried to call you, but your line was always busy."

"Dad was on the phone a lot. Oh, and I finally talked to Todd. He's gonna come down in a few weeks and stay a day or two."

I leaned off the bench, picked up an alfalfa pellet, and tossed it toward some sparrows.

"So you told Mitch."

Leslie shoved both hands in her back pockets. She might have been wearing old clothes, but they sure fit her in a new way.

"Yeah. But Todd has to sleep at your house, okay? Dad says there isn't enough room at our place."

"My house? Why my house? I don't want some vulnerable guy in the same room with me all night. Let him sleep on the floor."

"Are you kidding?"

"Why not? I've slept on your floor a hundred times."

"That's different."

"Oh, fine. 'Why don't you just curl up there in the cinders, Graham, while I tuck Sensitive Todd into the big, warm bed?'" I shook my head. "Sorry, Leslie. My place is out."

"Well, where's he going to stay?"

"How do I know? A hotel, maybe."

"I can't afford to pay for a hotel."

"I thought his father had money."

"Graham, Todd's gonna be my guest. I can't say, 'Welcome to Mariposa. There's the Hilton. Where's your credit card?' Graham, please."

Leslie looked just too pitiful. She even had her hands woven together like she was praying.

"All right. All right. But I have to ask Mom first. And I'm telling you this right now: if he gets sensitive and vulnerable with me in the middle of the night, he'll be sorry."

"He's nice. You'll like him."

"And tell him to leave his guitar downstairs. I don't want to wake up and hear him playing 'Malagueña' in the moonlight."

Just then we heard the track announcer, probably more than half a mile away, say, "They're off!" We listened, knowing our fathers were up there in the stands, binoculars right to their eyes. Working. Doing business. Making a living.

"By the way," she said when the crowd noise had faded away, "Todd sent me something."

"Be still my beating heart."

She grinned at me; her hair — turned blond from the

sun like mine never did — hung in long, loose curls like busted clock springs.

"Want to see it?"

"Not especially."

"Wait here."

I watched her run to the office, reach inside the door for something — something big — and run back. Then she handed it to me.

"It's a picture," she said.

I took the heavy manila mailer and reached inside. "It's an X ray," I said, sliding it out.

"Isn't it cool!"

It was just like a skeleton at Halloween, or at least half a skeleton: the long thigh bones, the hip sockets, and the pelvis, which looked like some kind of weird bat. "Why is he sending you a picture like this?"

"So I could have it." She pointed to a scrawl in one corner. "Look, he signed it."

I tilted my head. "Even my bones miss you," it said.

"This isn't sensitive. This is weird."

She looked around and slid the X ray back into its envelope. "No, it's not. It's cute. Just don't tell Dad, okay?"

"What am I gonna do, run in and tattle? 'Mr. Mitchell, Mr. Mitchell, Leslie's got a picture of a naked pelvis!'"

Leslie leaned over and started to pound on her legs with both fists, working her way around one and then starting on the other. "My thighs are fat," she announced.

"Those guys at the beach the other day sure didn't think so."

She finished the other leg anyway, and straightened up, panting a little. "And guess what I just found on my lip — a hair!"

"Whose?"

"Mine! I could be growing a mustache."

"I don't see anything," I said.

"I pulled it out. I want you to look every day, okay? The last thing I want to do is have a beard when Todd comes down."

"Think it over. He's probably too sensitive to have one, so it might be up to you."

Leslie rolled her eyes, then plopped onto a bench, pulling me down beside her.

"You know how some trainers will get themselves a little old colt with no bloodlines or conformation and pretend he's something special?"

"Uh-huh." My dad thought that's what kept some horses from ever developing — piling all those dreams on them so early.

"Well, do you think that's what I'm doin' with Todd?"

"Probably."

"Oh, bull. What do you know?"

"Gee, Leslie. You asked."

She sighed, staring down at the ground between her knees. "Do you practice your expressions sometimes? In the mirror, I mean. You know, like making a long, droopy face or a perky one or whatever."

"No, but I'll bet you do."

"Sometimes, if I'm alone. Because I want them to be just right when I need them." She glanced up at me. "I think boys make me do stuff like that. Todd especially, but boys in general. I think I might be boy-crazy. Do you think I'm boy-crazy?"

"Why don't you just be yourself?"

"Rather than crazy, you mean?"

"Rather than practicing, I mean."

She scooted closer and inspected my hurt lip. "I missed you," she said. "Don't go away for more long weekends, okay?"

"One Fourth of July at Grandma's was enough. She let me light one sparkler, but only if I stuck it in the ground and then stood about ten blocks away."

Leslie got up and tugged at me. "I'm finished over here. Want to go see Pepperoni?"

"Already did, but she asked about you."

Playfully she shoved me toward the barn, and a minute later we were unhooking the webbing in front of Pepperoni's stall. The filly shied a little, then leaned forward, sniffing us.

"Hi, girl." Leslie stepped inside and hunkered down. I reached for a set of curry combs and a hoof pick, just in case she'd picked up a stray pebble, and we both worked hard for a few minutes, each of us taking one side of her.

"Remember," I asked, straightening up and feeling my lip pound, "being out at the ranch when they were breaking her?"

Leslie's voice came from under the big, hard belly. "Uh-huh. What about it?"

"Nothin', I guess."

But I kept thinking about it anyway. About the whole process. How they put young horses on what they call the long lines, so trainers can make them do what they want. I'd told my dad once that I didn't like how all the wild parts got smoothed away.

After a while he'd said, "It's nice to think that stallions would run around Colorado with a big band of mares and every evening get up on a rise and paw the air like Flicka, but it's not true. Especially with thoroughbreds. We've bred them until they're not good for much except racing. So now we're responsible. They do their best for us, so we're obliged to do our best for them. That's the thing to think of, son. Not whether they'd be happier some other way."

"Graham?" said Leslie.

"Hmm."

Leslie walked around to my side. "What are you thinking about?"

Whether I'd be happier some other way. But I said, "How I don't like it that she had to be saddle-broke."

"Shoot, she took right to it. Victor said she caught on just like that, remember?"

"Yeah."

But still — broken. What a word. And for what? To stand around in a stall hour after hour, day after day?

Leslie nudged me, so I gave her a leg up. She sat backward on the horse, like a guy straddling the peak of a roof, and, scooting a foot or so at a time, worked on the places we couldn't reach from the ground. Finally she tossed me the brushes and, turning around, draped herself across the filly, looking like the wounded Indian scout in just about every old cowboy movie. But she wasn't wounded. She was grinning down at me.

"Ever want to be a jockey?" she asked, pulling her legs up short enough for stirrups.

"No way I could tack a hundred and fifteen pounds for the rest of my life."

As Leslie swung one leg over and slipped to the ground, she said, "I might make the weight, but it's too scary." She shook her head. "Anyway, I'd rather be the guy who tells the jockey what to do."

Just then Pepperoni heard something and stepped up to peer out of her stall. I muttered, "I guess, but when a rider gets off his horse in the nightcap, he's done. When you train, you're responsible for everything. All of it. All the time."

Leslie eyed me. "Well, you're gloomy all of a sudden." Then she frowned and peered outside, too. She held up one wait-and-see finger. "Hear those guys arguing? If it's those dumb grooms scarin' your Dad's horses, he's gonna fire their butts."

I cocked my head. "Doesn't sound like grooms to me. No Spanish."

"We'd better go see."

Instead, it came to us. We'd barely ducked under the webbing and straightened up when my dad, Mitch, and Mr. DiFiero came around the corner and stormed our way. Dad was in the lead, but the other two were closing fast on the outside.

"Take her!" My dad was trying to keep his voice down, but it just made his face red. "Put a shank on her right now and just take her."

"What's going on?" I said, not liking the sound of things at all.

Nobody answered me. The three grown-ups stopped. Dad and Mr. DiFiero faced off. Mitch hung back a little, looking at the ground.

"Dad?"

"Stay out of this, son." His eyes never left his best client.

Mitch put one hand out. "Leslie, come over here, honey."

But she just reached for my shirtsleeve, and we both sank back toward Pepperoni's stall.

Mr. DiFiero's white hands were sort of sculpting the air, patting it into the shapes he wanted, as he said, "Now, John. There's no reason to get upset."

"Look, Warren, you come over here saying all you want to do is ask about one of your horses, but you bring along another trainer. So what's the difference what I say? You might as well be holding a halter and a lead rope."

"Take it easy now. We were on our way someplace else. It's a coincidence Mitch is even with me."

Dad asked Mitch if that was true.

"About ten minutes ago, he asks me if I want a cup of coffee. I say okay, and we start out talking about the ninth race and how much the winner paid, when all of a sudden we take a hard right, and the next thing I know you two are arguing about Pepperoni."

Mr. DiFiero tried to look innocent. "On the way to the cafeteria it occurred to me this might be a good time to get a second opinion on that filly."

"A second opinion? We're not talkin' about a bellyache here. We're talking about a horse whose entire future you want to put on the line just so you can sound off to your friends about how you won a big-stakes race with a two-year-old."

"Is that what you think of me, that I'm just some drug-store cowboy who likes to show off?"

Leslie and I watched Dad look at Mr. DiFiero — at his snakeskin boots, at his bolo tie with the scorpion cinch, at the good-guy white hat without so much as a thumbprint on it, at his soft gloves with the tops rolled back to show off a watch about as big as an Oreo.

My father took a deep breath. When he spoke his voice wasn't as loud. "I've been trainin' for you for quite a while as these things go. We've always talked about what to do with your stock, especially the two-year-olds.

You want to see 'em all run as soon as possible, and I understand that; after all, you pay the bills. But I've told you before, and I'm telling you now: it doesn't work that way. Two horses foaled in the same month won't mature the same at all." He pointed to Leslie and me. "They'll be as different as these two kids."

Mr. DiFiero slithered toward my dad. "But isn't that the point, John? Isn't that precisely why I'm here? I believe that Pepperoni is way ahead of the other two-year-olds. If any of them run, I think it should be her."

Mitch stepped forward. "I'm gonna bow out of this, fellas." He turned to DiFiero. "I want to believe we were really going for coffee, Warren. I don't want to believe you got me over here under false pretenses."

"Would you train Pepperoni for me if I asked you?"

Mitch stepped back and put both hands up as if he had to push a piano uphill. "No way."

"He's gonna take her, Mitch," Dad said, sounding like he'd been up all night. "He made up his mind a long time ago. And I'd rather you had her than somebody else."

"John, I couldn't."

"Then I'll just find somebody," Mr. DiFiero said, "who needs the money more than you do."

Mitch snorted. "There's not enough hours in your busy schedule to locate that poor devil."

"So it's a deal then?"

When he held out his hand, Mitch looked at it, then at Dad, then at Leslie. Then me.

"I wish you wouldn't do this, Warren," my dad said.

Right then Mr. DiFiero stepped past him and put his arm around my shoulders.

"Look, Graham," he said, "you know this horse. You stood out there at my ranch in Riverside and named her. You've seen her a hundred times; she's your favorite, isn't she? What do you think? She's ready to run, isn't she?"

"Leave Graham out of this, Warren. He's just a kid."

"He's young, but I'd like to hear what he's got to say." He turned to me again. "Graham?"

When I stepped forward, Leslie took hold of my belt like I was walking into quicksand.

"I think she wants to," I said, fighting to keep my voice steady.

Mitch cocked his head and frowned. My dad stared, then turned away.

Mr. DiFiero reached for me. For a second he pulled my shirt while Leslie pulled my belt. Then she let go.

"Why is that, son? Why do you think she wants to run?"

With him hunkered down like that, I was taller, and I could smell his after-shave. I felt like the star in one of those old orphanage movies where some grown-up is forever bent over to get a good look at the merchandise. I didn't look at Mr. DiFiero, though; I looked up at my dad even though he was still staring the other way, his huge shoulders heaving.

I swallowed hard. "Well, I see Pepperoni almost

every day; Leslie and I both do. And I know she's dead tired of standing in that stall."

"And you've got a hunch about her, right?" Mr. DiFiero asked.

"Yeah, but more than that." I touched my chest. "Deeper than just a hunch."

"He's a kid, for God's sake," Dad said in a voice that made me cold all over. Then he looked at me. "You see her at her best and whenever you want to, when you're done surfing or taking a nap. I see her tired out; I see her favoring her right front leg sometimes; I see her —"

"And when's she going to be perfect, huh?" I asked, starting to shake. "When's everything going to be exactly right? When are you just gonna let go of her?"

When Dad didn't answer, Mr. DiFiero straightened up and nodded at Mitch, who more or less slunk over and took down a lead rope.

Dad had backed up a step or two and leaned against the wall. He crossed his arms and glared down at me. I tried to glare back, but I couldn't take it. If he'd been one of those video-game Masters of the Universe with the laser eyes, I'd have been nothing but a wisp of smoke.

$$\equiv \quad \equiv \quad \equiv$$

About a hundred yards from the ocean there was a pay phone.

"Need a quarter?" Leslie asked.

I felt for coins, shook my head, and stepped inside,

where there was almost as much sand on the floor as there was on the beach. She and I had called from here a hundred times for my mom to come pick us up. But not this time.

While the phone rang, I thought, *If I'm lucky, I'll get a wrong number.*

When Mom picked up, she was panting, so I asked if she was okay. For all I knew, both my folks were packing at top speed so they could light out for bigger and better racetracks and docile foster children.

"I'm fine. I've got that Jane Fonda tape on." I could almost see her blue sweatshirt.

"Is Dad home?"

"Yes."

"Is he still mad?"

"Are you kidding? And I don't blame him." I couldn't tell if she was sighing or just breathing hard from aerobics. "I know you're entitled to your opinions, but you could have picked a better time to express them."

"And get Pepperoni in trouble?"

"The way I heard it, she was already in trouble."

Outside, Leslie leaned into the glass and made her nose flat.

Turning around, I said, "I think I'll stay at Leslie's tonight." I moved the phone from one ear to the other. "I just don't feel like I belong at home right now."

My mom's voice faded a little, then came back. "Your father's not Godzilla. He's not going to come through the wall and eat your bed. He's just mad."

"It's just . . . maybe I want to think things over a little is all."

"I'd rather you came home."

"Well, I'd rather not." My hand started to sweat. "I'm just gonna be at Leslie's. I'll be home in the morning. I promise." I took a breath. "I know you guys are mad, but God, Mom, all I did was tell the truth. You drilled that into me, how important it is to always tell the truth."

I heard her breathing. "Maybe you're right. Let's talk about this in the morning, okay?"

I stared down at my feet, letting the sweaty phone slip a little. "I guess."

"Dad said your lip was all swelled up."

"He noticed?"

"What happened?"

"Just . . . I fell off my board."

"Put something on it, all right?"

"All right."

As I hung up, Leslie was nervously fiddling with the folding door, so I opened it. She stepped halfway in and looked around.

"Everything okay? You took long enough."

"Everybody's mad at me. If Fluffy was there she'd have hissed into the phone." I stared west.

"Would you like to be out there right now?"

"A little. The thing about surfing is that there's no Dad telling me which wave is ready, and no Mom saying there's something about the ocean she wants me to think about. *I* decide, and, okay, I fall off sometimes, but not every time. Either way, it's up to me."

"Do you like it better than you like horses?"

"I'm not sure about anything tonight, Les. For all I know I like to surf just because Dad can't."

Leslie felt for my hand and squeezed, tugging a little so I'd stop staring and start walking. "I thought your dad was gonna bust when you told DiFiero that Pepperoni wanted to run. Man, he was red all over. Even his hands were red."

"I think they wanted to be around my neck."

We'd started up the sidewalk that ran for miles along the beach. To our right, a little way off, was the Pacific. On our left were the houses with the million-dollar views, each with a huge picture window.

Inside, people were starting to have dinner or drinks, watch TV, or read. Little kids were kneeling on the floor playing with toys. Some of them were probably making plastic horses race in circles. When we passed a man looking down at his son and shaking his finger at him, Leslie asked, "Do you think you stood up to your father partly because he called you a little kid?"

I shook my head. "He didn't call me a little kid; he just called me a kid. And the answer is still no. I really think she's ready."

"Well, for what it's worth, she sure *looks* ready."

When we came to another corner, she pulled me uphill. We left the lighted streets, angling down other, dimmer ones. The TVs here were louder than at the beach. People were mostly sitting outside drinking beer, but they didn't have a view of the ocean, just of each other and cars up on blocks.

We headed for a small market, its windows glowing from neon beer signs. I could read the name above the door: EL MERCADO MARAVILLOSO.

I stopped her as she reached for the wooden handle.

"What if I'm wrong about Pepperoni? This morning I thought I was ready to surf with the big guys, and we know what happened then."

Leslie's complexion changed color each time a different sign flashed on. She tipped her hat back, wiped her dry nose on the back of one hand, and said, "Yeah, but that was just like an impulse or something. It's different with Pepperoni."

"I sure hope so."

Inside, two or three people working at the front spoke to her: "*Hola*, Leslie." She led me between them and up one narrow aisle.

"What's it mean?" I asked. "*El Mercado* whatever."

"*Maravilloso*? The Wonderful Market."

"Modest, aren't they?"

She shrugged. "It's close to home."

Just then something shiny and short rustled in the shadows.

"Jeez. What's that?"

"Oh, that's Pepe."

"A chicken named Pepe?"

"He's a rooster, actually. And don't shoplift anything. He'll bite you in the butt."

"You mean he's a security chicken?"

Just then somebody called, and Pepe stalked by majestically. I saw Leslie turn a corner, but I just stood there for a second, under the bare light bulbs, beside big chains of red chilis, on the wooden floor with its warped boards.

It came to me that I'd been around Hispanic people my whole life on the backstretch and didn't know ten words of Spanish, had never been in this market or any like it, knew zip about the Mexican grooms and hot walkers who worked for my folks. Where had I been all these years, anyway — surfing and taking naps like Dad said?

I found Leslie talking to the butcher, a big guy in a T-shirt with a tattooed heart way up on his biceps and under it a bunch of girls' names. All but the last one, Lupe, had a line tattooed through it.

When we nodded hello to each other, he asked Leslie something. She answered him in Spanish. He looked impressed, wiped one hand on his apron, held it out, and I shook it. Then he wrapped up a pork chop and we headed for the cash register.

"What did you say about me?" I asked.

"That you were an expert with horses. She rolled her r's: *Uno brujo*. A wizard."

I crossed my fingers. "With one horse, maybe."

At the checkout counter, a little kid about two was

sitting at the end of the conveyer belt with the groceries as if he'd been picked off a shelf, too. He was chewing on half a sandwich, sharing it with Pepe.

"Only one pork chop?" I asked, helping Leslie unpack the cart.

"Yours. We've got three at home."

"Let me pay, okay?"

She looked at the things laid out in front of us. Then she half-closed her eyes and added, lips moving just a little. Finally she frowned.

"I'm afraid you're gonna have to. I'm short." She shook her head. "If some horses I know had longer noses, Dad and I'd be millionaires."

≡ ≡ ≡

Leslie stopped in front of the Tiki Arms, handed me the second bag of groceries, and dug in her pocket for keys.

"This is where you guys stayed last year, isn't it?"

She shook her head. "Tiki Palace. Down about a block."

I studied the huge, dark, Polynesian totem poles with the frowning gods. Big torches stuck out of the ground at an angle, sputtering and hissing. The entrance was decorated with fake bamboo and looked like the way into some carnival ride with a name like Jungle Doom.

Inside the unlocked security gate was a tiny pool with a chaise longue half-sunk in the shallow end. All the pool toys had lost a lot of air, so they looked sick — a squishy shark, a droopy swan, an octopus with shriveled legs.

As we crossed the courtyard, climbed the stairs, and made our way along the balcony, I couldn't help but look through the open doors. Inside each apartment, blue light from the TV filled the room. Between gunshots, car crashes, and baseball games, people on commercials begged for more stuffing, real orange juice, or a secure future fixing computers.

"Do you think Mitch would give me a job working with his horses?"

"I'll bet he's not gonna want to come between you and your dad."

"You could already put the whole town of Mariposa between me and my dad. What's a few more feet?"

Leslie boosted her bag of groceries higher. "Well, the INS did come by a couple of days ago and take two of our grooms back to Mexico."

"So you think I should ask him?"

"Why not? Donna and I could use some help, and it'd be fun to work together. But don't get your hopes up." Then we stopped at number fifty-five. One of the numbers was missing, so there was a brass 5 and next to it a pale, ghost 5. "Home sweet apartment," she said.

Inside, everything that could be was bamboo, fake bamboo, or imitation fake bamboo. A path worn into the green carpet wound from the door past the bamboo coffee table and got lost in the hall.

"Me Leslie," she grunted. "You Graham."

"My mom had a book about this stuff," I said, nodding toward just about everything. "It's valuable in some weird way. Authentic California or something."

"Probably the guy who wrote it never lived here for more than twenty minutes. Just watch your step in the kitchen. We've got armed roaches. If I spray them, they spray me back."

We put the stuff down and started to fix dinner, something we'd done dozens of times: I opened cans and unwrapped things while she got out a skillet and some pans.

"Where's the napkins and stuff?"

"Donna'll do that."

"Is she over all the time now?"

"Enough so she's got her own chores."

"While Mitch watches. How do you get that job?"

Leslie shrugged. "My dad says cowboys don't do housework." She poked the sizzling pork chops and covered the yellow pan with a red lid. "Todd would help, I bet."

I cut some iceberg lettuce into quarters and put them into bowls. "Is Todd vegetarian?"

"All he ever ate when we went out was cheeseburgers."

"Then he can't be all bad."

Leslie fiddled with the burners for a second. "These'll be okay. I'll be right back."

When she disappeared into the bathroom, I went and sat on the couch. On the wall behind me hung a net decorated with glass floats, corks, and plastic fish hanging by their tails. The coffee table was stacked with old racing forms.

Man, was I tired! Maybe I should have gone into training to fight with my dad — you know, worked my way up through bickering and spats to the real thing.

Kicking off my boots, I stretched out. I could hear the TV from next door and, from underneath, the steady thud of the stereo. It sounded a little like drums. I guess that the bamboo and the leafy upholstery on everything was what nudged me into a dream where I was boiling in a big black cast-iron pot and my dad with a bone in his nose was dancing around licking his chops and muttering.

No, wait, it was Leslie who was muttering. And her father. And Donna. All standing in the kitchen. I got up and wandered in, trying to rub the sleep out of my eyes.

Mitch was pouring rum from a small greenish bottle into his glass and Donna's. Then he added soda pop from a gallon jug with COLA written on it. He caught my eye and lifted the glass in a toast.

"Be careful what you pray for," he said. "You might get it."

"I didn't pray to get in trouble, Mitch."

"Wasn't talkin' about you."

Donna took a sip of cola and said, "He always wanted to train for Mr. DiFiero."

"But," Mitch said, taking off his hat and sailing it across the room, "not this way and not this horse."

Then he walked over to the answering machine, pressed a button, and listened to his messages, writing notes on the back of an envelope. I leaned against the wall, feeling like a fifth wheel, and watched Donna set the table with silverware and some gray paper napkins. Everything she wore was tight. If she'd had a dime in her jeans I could have read the year it was minted. Her white western shirt looked ready to explode. A black belt with her name on the back was pulled tight as a cinch. Even her shoes — little straw-looking platform things — were bulging.

"Graham?" Mitch said.

I jumped, feeling guilty, then followed the worn path through the bamboo to the couch. He looked toward the kitchen and half-whispered, "What do you know about this Todd that Leslie's been talkin' about?"

"Not much."

"Did you know he sent her a picture of his crotch?"

"It was an X ray."

"I know what it was, and it's still a picture of his crotch."

"I think it was supposed to be a joke or something."

He frowned. "Maybe." He motioned for me to sit down. "He's not some drugged-out pervert, is he?"

"Gee, no. He's some kind of sensitive musician. It sounds to me like he can't go outside without a sweater."

He looked at his daughter and Donna, standing side by side at the sink. "When he comes down here to visit, keep an eye out, okay?"

"In case he faints?"

"You know what I mean, Graham."

"Yes, sir."

He settled back, picked up the new racing form, and began to read the front page.

"Mitch? If I asked you for a job, would you give me one?"

He lowered the paper. "Are you asking?"

"Yes."

He let a breath out slowly. "What's your dad gonna say?"

That made me grit my teeth. "How come what he wants is always more important than what I want?"

"He's your dad, Graham."

"Yeah, but forever?"

A fraction of one corner of his mouth turned up in what had to be the world's smallest grin. I took it as a sign and scooted closer.

"Look, I want to be around Pepperoni. I'm good for her. And what's good for her is good for you, right?"

He squinted. "How old are you now, anyway?"

"Fourteen next month."

"If I say yes, and I'm not dead sure I will, but if I do, you'd have to work."

"Mitch, I've always worked."

"No, son. You've always been around. It ain't the same."

≡ ≡ ≡

While Leslie, Donna, and I did dishes, Mitch took the cover off a portable record player that'd been hidden behind a pretty bad imitation of a banana tree. Then he grabbed a footstool and rummaged around in the top of a closet. He finally climbed down holding a box with GALLO WINE printed on the side. Out came a stack of records.

"What are those?" I asked.

"Old 78s," Leslie said. "Ever seen one?"

"I'm not sure."

She dried her hands on a dish towel with one burned edge and led me into the living room.

"Can I show Graham?" she asked, leaning over her dad.

"Sure, sugar."

Each one was in a reddish envelope of its own with a hole in the middle so you could read the label. She pointed at the title, "Mood Indigo," then handed it over.

"It's heavy," I said holding it, as she did, by the edges.

"Play this one," she said, and her dad took it so slowly it was like we were handling donor organs.

Then Leslie tugged at my shirt, and we drifted back into the kitchen to finish up. Mitch crouched next to the little square Motorola until the music started. Then, as if he was following the notes as they flowed out of the speaker, he stood up, pushed the drape to one side, and stared out into the courtyard. The songs were scratchy-sounding, like something out of a black-and-white movie. And sad in a way.

Donna drifted over and stood by Mitch, leaning against him, one arm around his waist, her thumb hooked in his black belt with the turquoise inlay.

When Mitch leaned down to turn a record over, Leslie whispered, "He always does this when he's thinking about something."

"Maybe whether to give me a job or not."

She nodded. "And about Pepperoni, probably, and what it means if she stays sound."

If?

Just then Donna said something to him, so he bent down and paged through his records.

"Did he collect those himself?" I asked.

"Oh, no. Grandad left him those."

I almost asked, "Is that all?" But I'm glad I caught myself. First of all, it was rude. Second, it was none of my business. And last, what if it was all? Maybe it was enough. Anybody could see those records meant a lot to him.

I dried a spatula, a frying pan, and a kids' bowl, one

with a smiling bear on the bottom so you could eat down through your cereal and finally smile back.

I'd just hung up the damp dish towel when their phone rang, and the mood — Leslie and me whispering, the old-fashioned music in the background, the thickish light from one little bulb in its bamboo-colored shade — was broken.

Leslie held the receiver out to her dad and said she'd be first in the bathroom. Mitch started to talk to somebody, calling him mister, so it was probably a client; Donna drifted toward the table and sat down, glancing at me as she settled in.

"Your dad's winnin' some races." She picked up her left foot with both hands, slipped the shoe off, and winced as she started to massage.

"Yeah." I grabbed the dish towel again, dried a dry glass, then, feeling like I was about to break something, just sat down, too.

Donna kept both eyes on her sore foot. "How's your mom?"

"She's fine."

"Tell her I said hi, will you?"

"Uh-huh."

"She has got the most beautiful hair. Looks like it's on fire all the time, and it's thick as a turf course." Then she eyed me as if I'd been marked down from seventy-five dollars. "You got her eyes and his nose."

"At least there's something that's not Dad's."

She put one foot down and reached for the other. "Your dad was about the best boss I ever had: worked you hard, paid you good, and never tried nothin' funny. And I just loved the way he took care of his stock. I'd still be there if I hadn't gone up north."

I glanced at the clock. That's what he'd be doing right now, making the night inspection, going from stall to stall until he came to the empty one where Pepperoni used to be.

I didn't like thinking how nice my dad could be, and I was pretty sure he wasn't making a list of *my* good qualities.

"How many horses has Mitch got?" I blurted out.

Donna shook her hair a little. "Fifteen now, with the new filly."

"You and Leslie do most of the work yourselves?"

"Lately, anyway." Then she parted her hair and leaned toward me. "Are my roots black?"

I shook my head and told a little lie: "Pure palomino."

She laughed a little as I heard the shower go off. I looked that way, then toward the hall where Mitch was still talking.

"How long have you worked at the track?" I asked.

Donna teased me. "Are you trying to find out how old I am?"

"I just feel weird tonight. And I guess I'd rather talk than not."

She reached for my hand and patted once. Hard. "Honey, you're just gonna spend the night and go home tomorrow, and everything'll be all right."

I took a big breath and let it out. "Did Mitch tell you what happened?"

"Sure."

"And?"

She looked at me, still massaging one foot. Then she shrugged.

"Does that mean you don't think I did the right thing?"

"Not for me to say. The only thing I know is that everybody fights with their parents. It's part of growin' up."

"Do Leslie and Mitch fight?"

"Do fish pee in the ocean?"

"I hope not. I surf every day."

Donna laughed, the lines around her eyes curving upward. "And as for how long I've been around racetracks, I started when I was sixteen, younger than that, actually."

"You're kidding. Didn't you go to school?"

"Oh, off and on. My uncle had some horses, and I started rubbin' 'em for him one summer. Then when he went north for the Stockton meet, I went along. Pretty soon the only place I really felt at home was on the backstretch."

"What about your parents?"

She frowned at her big, rough hands — first one side

and then the other — like they were things she was thinking about taking back to the store.

"Oh, they were around, but I didn't want much to do with 'em. My mom was all right most of the time, but Smitty was just trash."

Leslie came out of the bathroom wearing baggy blue pajama bottoms and a T-shirt with SURFERS RULE on it.

"Your turn," she said to me. "I'll get out the sleeping bags."

Right about then Mitch came around the corner. "Wilson wants us to add a horse or two to his stable." He looked pleased, touching Donna's hair, glancing at Leslie and me. "Maybe this is my lucky day, after all."

Donna reached for her shoes. "You two sleep now, hear? Don't talk all night."

She and Mitch walked toward the door. "I'm gonna lock this, Leslie, okay?"

"Yes, sir. We're not goin' anywhere."

When the lock clicked, I asked, "Does she ever stay over?"

Leslie shook her head. "It just takes him about four hours to drive her home sometimes."

"Maybe her apartment's in Arizona."

Leslie grinned. In that long, silly T-shirt, with her hair pulled back, she looked really young.

I pointed. "I'll just wash up a little. You can throw my sleeping bag anywhere."

"Use the blue toothbrush if you want. It's mine."

When I came out of the bathroom a few minutes later, all the lights were off.

"Over here," Leslie said, turning on a little flashlight and pointing the way.

Her room was at the opposite end of the hall. One sleeping bag was stretched to the edge of the door. The other was laid out at a right angle in the hall.

"My room's a mess. This is okay, isn't it?"

I said, "Sure," as she worked the long zipper and slid in.

"I'll turn the light off so you can undress."

"Okay."

So I slipped my pants off, then got into the other bag and squirmed around a little to get settled. When I turned her way we were almost touching. I could smell the minty toothpaste she used.

"You okay?"

I told her I was.

"You sleepy?"

"Not yet. You?"

"A little, maybe."

I rolled to my left and put both hands behind my head. Leslie and I'd camped out a few times in my back-yard. But instead of constellations, this time there was only a narrow ceiling with some spots where the rain had leaked through.

"Donna's nice," I said, talking real soft. "But she's tough, too. One time when she was workin' for us, a horse stepped on her, and she just kept right on goin' until Dad sat her down. When he pulled her boot off, it was all full of blood."

"She and I get along pretty good."

"Do you ever wish they'd get married?"

I heard her sigh. "After Mom died, he was so sad, remember?"

"He was always calling my dad from some bar."

"Things are a lot better now. I know he likes Donna, and the only reason he takes her home is because he's so strict with me. But I wouldn't care if they lived together." I didn't hear her move at all, but suddenly her voice was closer. Warmer. "Would you live with somebody?"

"I don't know."

"Me neither."

Then she thrashed around a little, so I did, too. I had the old Yogi Bear sleeping bag, the one with a picture of Yogi stretched out with both paws folded on his chest and some big Z's hovering around his black nose. It was a little short for me, so I had to scrunch up to keep my shoulders warm.

"Graham? Remember when we were nine or so and we had those kitties?"

"What about 'em?"

"Remember what they did?"

"Yours kept beating mine up."

"No, when they were older."

Uh-oh. That again. "I'm alseep, Leslie. Deeply, deeply asleep. An earthquake couldn't wake me up."

"Graham, you're the only friend I've got with a . . . I mean you've got . . . Well, let's just say you're the only one I can ask about what really goes on, you know . . . down there."

"You sound like I've just moved to Australia."

"You know what I mean." We tossed around some more, ending up, both of us, on our backs, with our hair barely touching. "I know Todd wants me to do it with him."

My mouth went dry. My heart was throbbing.

"And I'm not sure I don't want to." Her face turned toward mine. "I will someday with somebody. And a couple of times I got so excited with him. But I could get pregnant, couldn't I?"

"Well, sure."

"I asked Todd once about birth control, and he just said not to worry. What's that supposed to mean?"

"Maybe he had condoms or something?"

"Maybe, but why didn't he tell me?" I felt her head shake. "There's something about it I don't like. 'Don't worry' isn't going to stop anything from happening."

She was breathing a little hard, sounding about half-mad. "Maybe it's shallow or stupid or not hip, but I want to be special to Todd. Not just some kind of experience he has." I felt her turn my way. "Do you think that's dumb?"

"Do you know that feeling I've got that Pepperoni is ready to run? Don't you have something like that about you and Todd?"

"Not yet." She slid one arm out of her sleeping bag and patted my hair. "So that's why I have to ask you embarrassing questions."

I reached for her hand and squeezed. Suddenly, she yawned. "I'm really glad you're here tonight."

"Me, too."

"Can you sleep?" She was almost out.

"I'll be fine."

"Think of something nice," she murmured. "Even when my mom was so sick, she'd always tell me, 'When you can't go to sleep, think of something nice, honey.'"

"All right."

"Graham, everything I just said is a secret, okay?"

"God, Leslie. Sure."

"Is there anything you want to ask me?"

"No, I have a penis; I know everything."

She giggled. "See you in the morning then."

I lay there in the dark, listening to Leslie breathe. Once she sighed a little and kicked, but when I rolled over and looked, she was dead to the world. Down the way a little, somebody slammed a door and laughed. I could barely hear a baby crying. Somebody else yelled, and then there was a thud. Pretty soon, I heard a key in the door, and Mitch slipped in.

I did, as a matter of fact, have something I wanted to ask Leslie. It was about Dad and what I'd thought that night on the bluff. But I was too ashamed.

≡ ≡ ≡

Next morning, feeling jittery on nothing but toast and orange juice, I walked home by myself right after Mitch and Leslie headed for the barns.

I cut down through the garage, picked up my surfboard, then climbed the stairs to the kitchen. Mom was working at the sink when I clattered in. She was wearing lime-green shorts and a blue sweatshirt with white lambs on it. Some trainers' wives got into the whole horse thing — horse earrings, horse bracelets, T-shirts with grinning stallions on them, personalized license plates saying FILLY #1. It was like Mom to wear a shepherd sweatshirt in horse country.

"Welcome home," she said, without turning off the water. "You okay?"

I shrugged, looked around. "Is he gone?"

"Uh-huh. Any news?"

"I think I'm going to work for Mitch."

She shook her head slowly and laughed without making any sound, one of those laughs that means nothing's actually funny. "Oh, that'll help."

I guess I wasn't in the mood for irony, because I snapped at her. "Well, at least I'm gonna get paid, and I'm not gonna run around after Dad like you do. God, he's got you balancing his books and answering his phone and I don't know what all. And for free!"

Mom wrung out a dishcloth until it was bone-dry, then turned around and crossed her arms. "Let's get one

116

thing straight, buster. I'm doing what I want to do, and I'm good at it. The fact is, if I wasn't handling the business end of this stable, I'd probably be doing it for some other trainer." She took a step toward me, and I scooted backward in my chair. "It really ticks me off when people think that I'm under my husband's thumb just because what I'm good at is good for him, too. We're in business together, Graham. Horse racing is a partnership, and this marriage is a partnership. But none of that means I'm not my own person."

I held up both hands. "Okay, okay. Lucky you. But I don't feel like *my* own person."

Mom took a deep breath. "Give yourself a little time."

I sat and rubbed at an invisible spot on the slick table while she smoothed the dishrag she'd strangled.

"I think I'll go to the beach for a while."

"Sit down for a minute first. There's something I want you to think about."

"You always say that!" All of a sudden I was upset again. Or still. "You always say, 'I just want you to think about this, honey.' If I was hitting cats with a hammer, you'd probably say, 'I want you to think about those kitties' headaches, Graham,' but we'd both know you really wanted me to stop."

She loomed over me. "You want straight talk? Okay, here's some straight talk: Are you sure all this is just about a horse? I've got a hunch it's you who wants to run. You're the one who wants to bust loose and be free, but you've got it worked out so they're only the filly's feelings and not yours."

"I know she's ready to run! I don't know how I know, but I do. Why won't anybody believe me?"

Then I slumped and rubbed my face like I'd just come out of the ocean. Mom sat down across from me, reached for my hand, covered it with hers, and squeezed. She had lots of freckles, even on her fingers. Once when I was little she'd let me connect some with a ballpoint pen, and I made a star, a little house, and a chicken. Everything had sure been easy then!

"I'm confused almost all the time," I told her.

I must have looked so glum, she let up a little. "I know being a teenager is tough. You're just gonna have to give yourself some time. You're changing, Graham."

"Sure, but into what, a horse killer?"

She shifted in her chair. "I don't want to sound callous, but horses get put down all the time. Sometimes it's just the way things are. Sometimes it's actually somebody's fault. Either way, the day goes on."

"But what if this time it's *my* fault?"

"There's not a mean bone in your body, Graham." She looked at me intently. "You'd never do anything on purpose to hurt anybody or anything."

All of a sudden my chest hurt so bad, I winced. "I do, too, have mean bones in my body. Lots of them." I couldn't stop myself. Big hot tears were leaking out of my eyes. "I thought the worst thing about Dad that anybody could think. Ever. And I thought it twice. I didn't want to, but I couldn't help myself." I leaned forward and put my forehead against the gray Formica table top. I was hot all over.

I could feel Mom studying me, not in a cold, scientific way, just patiently. "Take your time," she said softly. "You don't even have to tell me if you don't want to."

"I do want to, though." I looked up at her, my jaw quivering. "I want to tell somebody. Leslie and I were talking last night, and I couldn't even tell her."

Mom got up and ran a glass of water for me. I put both hands around it, as if I was five and working hard on not spilling things. "I wanted him to . . ." I started but couldn't finish. It was like I couldn't say the word. It stuck in me somewhere. I looked at my mother, but everything was blurry. I moved my lips, but almost no sound came out.

"You wanted your dad to die, is that right?"

"Yes." Boy, I really started in then — I even cried in my glass of water. Mom let me quiet down. She watched me swallow, blow my nose, wipe at my eyes. Finally I said, "Once down by the bluff a few weeks ago. And then again last night in the barn. I was mad, and I just wished that he was gone. Invisible. Dead."

"Ah," she said, nodding slowly. "That."

"Yeah." I wiped my eyes on one sleeve. "That."

"You know, don't you, that everybody thinks that at one time or another."

"Oh, bull."

"I did."

I'd laid my head on my crossed arms, but that made me look up. "No way. About who?"

"My folks — who else? I'd yell, 'I hate you. I hate you. And I wish you were dead.'"

I took a sip. "You said that to Grandma?"

"She wasn't *my* grandma. She was the insensitive, callous, and hopelessly behind-the-times woman who'd stolen me away from the Queen of the Gypsies, my real mother. But then I wanted my dad to die, too, sometimes. I was an equal opportunity brat."

"What'd they do?"

"Got mad. Laughed at me. Different things. They never made me feel too guilty. Looking back, I'm grateful for that."

I sniffed and tugged at my T-shirt. "Are you sure everybody thinks this stuff? Schoolteachers? The pope?"

She nodded. "Everybody was a kid once. And, anyway, the point is that nobody dies. We're not that powerful. We just end up feeling bad."

I looked into her ocean-green eyes. "Don't tell Dad, okay?"

"Okay."

I walked over to the sink and splashed water on my face. I felt better — drained but not so flat-out tired. When I circled Mom, I ran my hand along the back of her chair. She reached up to pat my arm, then pushed away from the table, leaned to kiss me on the forehead, and got to her feet. "Well, this half of the partnership's got things to do — computers to stare at, owners to bill, and purse money to divide up. What about you?"

"I might go surf." I stood up and stretched, walked over, and ran one hand down the turquoise arc on my board. "I wish you could come with me."

She laughed. "That's just what you need with those big saltwater studs out there by the pier — your mother in her paisley one-piece Jantzen."

"I wouldn't care."

"I know you wouldn't," she said. "And that's just one of about ten thousand things I like about you."

≡ ≡ ≡

I felt a little better by the time I rode my bike over to the track that afternoon. Talking to Mom'd helped a lot, and the Pacific had cleared out most of the rest.

Usually I just paddled out there and took my place in the food chain. But every now and then I knew what those guys who got mystical about surfing meant — waiting, straddling my board, facing west with the everyday world behind me, sometimes I'd find myself breathing with the ocean. Every little swell a breath. Not just balanced on the water, but part of the water.

I'd no more than walked through the gate marked CREDENTIALS, though, than my mood slipped again, and I wasn't the only one. Stepping around a couple who were already arguing about who'd lost the bankroll and why, I barely bumped into an old guy who groused and batted at me with his program like I was a giant fly. And sitting on the long green benches were sad-looking people, kind of stunned or tired or counting their crumpled bills and separating the nickels from the pennies from the lint. It looked like everybody'd had a bad night.

Just then Leslie, who'd been buried in her racing form, spotted me, hopped up, and trotted my way. She was wearing her second-best outfit — an almost-new Mariposa Downs T-shirt, jeans with creases, and black Tony Lamas from last Christmas.

"Todd's coming in three weeks and —"

"Like I didn't have the date marked on my calendar with a big skull and crossbones."

Leslie stuck out her tongue. "*And* Pepperoni's gonna run the day after that in the Solo Chico Stakes."

"Oh, jeez."

"Yeah. Dad put her name in this morning, right after his first fight with DiFiero."

"What'd they fight about?"

"There's a longer race right at the end of the meet against easier horses, but he wouldn't go for it."

"DiFiero wouldn't?"

"Exactly. He wants to win that stakes." I was shaking my head when Leslie added, "Have you seen my dad?"

I shook my head harder.

"Well, you go to work for us in the morning, if you still want to. He said to say so if I saw you first."

"All right!"

She held her hand out and, when I raised mine, slapped it gently.

"Speaking of dads, is mine around?"

"Somewhere." She glanced at the program. "He's got a horse pretty soon."

"I know."

"Didn't you talk to him yet?"

"I made sure it took about an hour to walk home from your place."

"I kept checking on Pepperoni this morning, and she's fine." We stepped off the sidewalk to let some guys by. "Mitch really doesn't want her in that short race, but DiFiero's got his mind made up."

"It's not smart to run young horses where they can't do pretty good. They start to think that coming in last is what racing's all about." I rubbed my tired eyes. "Or at least that's what Dad thinks."

Just then, like saying the word *Dad* had done the trick, there he was, coming in the same gate I'd used a few minutes earlier. I pointed.

"I guess I'd better talk to him. I guess that's what I really came for today."

Leslie waved toward my father. "See you upstairs?"

"If I come out of this in one piece. Anyway, tell Mitch I'll be by in the morning with my work clothes on."

Dad had seen us and slowed down. I made my way through the big Saturday crowd. People were dressed for sun, but the morning fog had never really burned away, so the girls in tank tops stood around with their arms crossed, and the old-timers looked at each other knowingly and zipped up their Members Only windbreakers.

My father was wearing a blue sport coat and slacks. Some bettors thought that when a trainer dressed up it meant he was counting on getting his picture taken in the winner's circle. I knew he and Mom were probably going out with a client after the races. Or all his jeans were dirty.

When I got close enough, he jammed both hands into his pockets. I saw him take a couple of breaths. Neither one of us knew what to say or do.

Somebody passed and spoke. Dad barely nodded. He hated to talk to people he didn't know very well. They were always after a tip, the hotter the better. As if Dad had talked to the horse, who'd said he was depressed and felt like running ninth.

Finally he started. "I hear you're workin' for Mitch."

"So?"

"Graham, you're my son. How does it look for you to be workin' with another trainer? What are people gonna think?"

"That's what's important, isn't it? What people think about you. What about me?"

"I meant both of us."

"Oh, sure."

Then he turned one way, and I turned the other. He looked beside me, and I looked past him. We heard the call to the post. He glanced toward the saddling paddock.

"Listen," I said finally, "I know you have to go. But I just —" This was getting hard. Words were collecting in my mouth, but they were all mixed up like an old Scrabble game. "I guess I just thought we ought to talk."

"What about?"

"So you're still really mad?"

He scanned the crowd. "Hell, yes. I'm mad, and I'm disappointed."

Suddenly he glared down at me. His eyes were so piercing I could barely stand it. I started to fiddle with my gold-colored cap.

"You need a haircut," he said.

I let that one go by. "Anything else?" I asked.

"Yeah. I feel betrayed, damn it." He leaned over me, shutting out the weak sun. "You and I've always been on the same side, but not last night, for damn sure, and not anymore since you're gonna work for Mitch."

"If I'm going to be around Pepperoni, I have to work for Mitch."

"You could've been around her and not lifted a hand if you'd just kept your mouth shut."

I let a couple of people slide past, waiting for some privacy. "I got Pepperoni into this."

"You're not responsible for that, Graham. DiFiero had his mind made up a long time ago."

"Maybe, but I still *feel* responsible, and I'm not gonna back away now."

He nodded. Barely. "I know that. And I'm not saying I don't admire the way you stuck up for what you thought was right." He stared down again. "For such a little twerp you've got some real *cojones*."

I watched his big hard stomach go up and down. He was still breathing like he was mad.

"Maybe you don't like me much right now," I said, "but I told the truth last night, and that's what you always said I should do."

"What'd I just say, Graham? I said I admired you, didn't I?"

"And then called me a little twerp."

I saw his jaw tighten. He wiped his sunburned forehead with one sleeve and frowned at the damp mark on his blue jacket.

"This gives me one giant headache, I'll tell you that."

Twenty yards away, horses for the next race wound their way from the receiving barn. We watched his — not *ours* anymore — whose name was Copy Book. Then he said, "A few new rules around the house, okay? I don't want you blabbing to Mitch about my stock; I don't want to hear about his. We'll find something different to talk about over dinner, maybe the weather. Another thing: you get yourself up in the morning and off to work. Your mom's not gonna do it. You understand?"

"Yes, sir."

He took a step, stopped, and turned back, frowning. "Is Mitch gonna pay you?"

"Well, sure, but —"

"Well, he'd bet on how many teeth a chicken'd have if a chicken had teeth, so don't gamble it all away. Give your mom some. Let her put it in the bank."

He spun on one heel, but I ran after him, cutting him off like a sports car would a van. "Wait a minute, okay? Just wait."

"I've got a horse to saddle."

Was I getting used to this or what? Nothing inside me was shaking. Even my voice was clear and hard, and for once it didn't threaten to break. "When Mitch pays me, it's my money. I can do what I want with it."

"So this is the thanks I get for givin' good advice."

"It wasn't advice. It was an order."

His eyes went to slits, and I knew he was grinding his teeth. In spite of myself, I took a step back, then another one. Then he just shook his head.

"I give up," he said, stalking away, knocking some guy off balance, who spun around, ready to start something, until he saw what he was up against.

PART THREE

$\equiv$On the morning of the Big Day — Leslie's Big Day, anyhow — she and I were sprawled on some hay bales. It was about noon, and we were finally done with our chores: done washing out buckets and wheelbarrows, done shoveling *el grosso* straw out of stalls, done saddling and unsaddling, done walking hot horses in circles until they'd cooled out, done watering horses, washing horses, scraping horses dry, done cleaning their bridles, halters, reins, and saddles, done laundering long bandages and hanging them out in the sun, done lugging bags of feed, done sweeping up, done studying horses' legs and coats, done brushing and currying, done feeling for heat in their ankles, done dodging a flying hoof or some angry, yellow teeth.

I pulled off the leather gloves my mom had found for me and flexed one aching hand.

"What's wrong?" Leslie said, looking at my palm.

"Baling wire kind of cut in when we were restacking that back room."

She spit on her finger and rubbed at the red line across my palm.

"Graham?"

"Hmmm?" I was tired, but it was a good tired. I liked looking at the spick-and-span barn and knowing I'd helped make it that way. I liked Leslie healing my wounds.

"Will you eat dinner with Todd and me tonight?"

I jerked my hand away and wiped it on my shirt. "No."

"Why not?"

"Because he sent *you* his X ray, not me."

She sat up and brushed loose straw off my sweaty T-shirt. "What's it called when you feel two different ways?"

"Ambivalent?"

"That's it. That's how I feel. It's great Todd's coming, but haven't you just loved the last three weeks? We work hard; then we go to the beach; then we go to the races."

"I'm still not gonna eat dinner with you guys. Take Donna and Mitch."

"Oh, sure. Are you going to leave the door open for him tonight at your house or what?"

"I'm sure not going to wait up in my robe and curlers. I'll get a key from Mom."

She put both hands on her legs and tugged at her jeans. "Do you think we should sit Todd in the boxes this afternoon or stand down by the rail?"

132

"I don't know and, can you believe it, I don't care."

"It'd be more authentic down by the rail."

"Fine, let's stand there. Maybe a horse'll come way wide and run over him."

She slapped me lightly with her rolled-up gloves. "I like it that you're jealous."

"Who's jealous? I'm just sick of hearing about him."

"Uh-huh."

As she took a crumpled list out of her pocket, I thought that I *was* sick of Todd this and Todd that. But sometimes I didn't mind talking about him because then I wasn't worrying about Pepperoni. Todd might or might not like the racetrack, might or might not be everything that Leslie wanted him to be. But he for sure wouldn't go lame and have to be put down.

"Who's that chestnut Dad just got?" Leslie asked, frowning at her grimy piece of paper with cross-outs and arrows all over it.

"Mission Hills. He's in the tenth stall."

"Damn. How come you can remember that stuff and I can't?"

"I told you, it's a trick. You just don't want to learn it."

"I can't."

"You never tried."

"Why should I try when I can't?"

"How do you know if you don't try!"

"Well, don't get mad."

I swung my legs over a broken bale and stood up. "Sorry," I muttered.

"Teach me, okay?"

I turned toward her. "I was going to go see Pepperoni."

"You see Pepperoni all the time. If this trick of yours is as easy as you said, how much time could it take from your precious day?"

"Now who's mad?"

Leslie leaned over to spit at a sparrow.

"Okay, okay," I said. When I held out one hand, she put hers in it. "Not that, the list."

"I can read my own list," she said, half-throwing it at me.

"Not anymore." I tore it in two and tossed it in a trash can. "Just listen, okay? What we're going to do is write a story with you in it. But exaggerated like crazy. The crazier the better."

"What are you talkin' about?"

"This memory trick Dad taught me." I tugged at her bare arm, and we sat down on the hay bales again. "The first horse in the first stall is Bootsy's News, right?" So you imagine you're wearing big boots with headlines all over 'em."

Leslie frowned.

I pointed at her feet. "Look down and picture them, okay?"

"I guess."

"Now the second horse is Basic Training, so what do you see?"

"Guys in the army?"

I shook my head. "*You* in the army. Maybe crawling under barbed wire with shells going off all over the place. And you're crawling toward what?"

She turned and looked toward the stalls. "Rice Bowl."

"How big?"

"Huge." She started to grin. "Is this all there is to it?"

"Just about."

"So I crawl past this giant rice bowl . . ."

"Maybe you claw your way to the top, and from up there you can see . . ."

She glanced again. "Clever King. A clever king, I mean, sitting on his throne. And he tells me to go past the hospital . . ."

"Which you can see from where you are, which is sitting in his lap."

"Right. And inside the hospital is Mama Heart." Leslie started to point to each horse. "From there I skip along the Road To Win, climb up on a stage, and sing a Chime Song to hundreds of cheering people."

"Good. And, look, you always know who's where. Like if Mama Heart is number five, you can run the story backward to remember who three is."

Leslie stuck the tip of her pink tongue out a little as she thought. "That'd be Rice Bowl, because I'd leave

135

Mama Heart in the hospital and go back past Clever King, who I saw from the top of the rice."

"Bingo."

"That is so great, Graham!"

We looked at each other, then around each other, then near each other, then at each other again.

"Who's great?" Mitch asked, coming around the corner.

"Graham is," Leslie said.

Mitch grinned his patented half-grin. "Well, does the great one want to walk down to the chute? I'm havin' Paco break Pepperoni out of the gate one more time."

"Me, too?" Leslie asked.

"Sure. Donna's already down there."

A few minutes later the four of us were leaning on the rail and watching some handlers school the last of that morning's young horses. They loaded them in sets of threes, then sprung the latch.

I was still suprised at the noise a starting gate made — riders yelling at the handlers and their horses, the bell that clanged as the gates slammed back. It was no wonder it took getting used to.

As Paco, Pepperoni's exercise rider, led her past, Mitch yelled, "Let her get a good look at Graham!"

So I took off my hat as if I was about to get my picture taken, and Pepperoni bobbed her big head.

Then she moved up to the gate and in. But when the bell rang, she came out last.

Mitch shook his head as Donna reached over and patted his forearm.

I said, "It wasn't that bad."

"Maybe not, but it wasn't good."

"She's just big, Dad," Leslie said.

I reran the scene in my mind. And wouldn't you know it — something that Dad had pointed out once made sense. So I said, "Maybe the handler was too rough with her. She's not used to that."

Mitch thought it over, then shrugged. "Worth a try. I'll tell the starter to put somebody in with her that ain't a sadist. She don't need to give the field two jumps right out of the box."

He patted Leslie and me on the shoulders, then took off with Donna.

I stared out across the track, which looked so smooth from the stands but was actually deep and, from three hours of workouts, cut up pretty badly. Then I said, "That was cool."

"What? Watching Pepperoni?"

"No. Having *any* dad ask me a question and then really listen to the answer."

"What was cool was how you saw she was being handled wrong."

"It's funny, but I feel like I really know more about horses now. And if I do it's just because I've been working with them every day. Not like before when I just sort of dropped by."

"That's how I learned," Leslie said. "It just kind of seeps in, the way people who make wine have purple feet."

I grinned at her, turned around, and let my head fall back. The sun was warm, and I felt a little sleepy.

"You look good with a tan," Leslie said.

I started to stutter. "Uh, I'm, uh, going to surf for a while. Want to come?"

Was I ever going to know what to say when girls told me something like that, or would I always be Mr. Clodnoggin?

"You're certainly good-looking, Graham."

"Uh, yup. But wait'll you see the water run out of my nose."

Leslie shook her head. "I'd better clean the apartment and take about three baths."

Oh, that. Oh, him.

Leslie felt it. "You're not going to get mad and leave me alone with Todd, are you, Graham?"

"I thought leaving you alone with him was the idea."

"One o'clock. You promised."

"All right, all right."

"For sure?"

"I said all right!" But I tossed it over my shoulder as I stalked away.

$$\equiv \quad \equiv \quad \equiv$$

At one o'clock sharp, Leslie and I were standing outside the main entrance to Mariposa Downs. She had a blue, shimmery shirt on, the same color as her eyes, her Guess? jeans, as new-looking as the first night I'd seen them in June, and her new red boots.

"Does this shirt look lumpy?" she asked as fans streamed by us. "I've got one of my dad's old T-shirts on underneath so I don't get stains under the arms. I don't want Todd to know I sweat."

"Well, if he gets me alone and asks me those questions that guys sometimes ask each other, your secret's safe with me."

"Would you want to fly five hundred miles to see somebody and then have her drip like a Popsicle?"

"Is this a trick question?"

The crowd poured off one of the track's green and white trams. Pretty soon there was nobody left except a couple of senior citizens and a skinny kid who looked like he'd taken the wrong bus at Hollywood and Vine — leather pants, silk scarves tied to his belt loops, a long sleeveless coat but no shirt, shades dark enough to wear *on* the sun, and a huge lampshade of bleached hair.

"There's another tram in ten minutes," I said.

"That could be Todd," she whispered.

Just then he spotted us — the kid in the leather pants, I mean — and loped our way.

This is sensitive? I thought. Exactly which part of Greece is this god from?

"No, it can't be," she muttered.

Todd whipped off his shades and held his skinny arms out. "Leslie! Hey, babe. You're here. All right."

I nudged her.

"Hi, Todd," she croaked.

Then his hands sort of slithered all over her, and he planted a big, smoochy kiss on her cheek.

"This is Graham," said Leslie, struggling to get away like someone in a creepy movie who's just been attacked by a hormonal fern.

"Hey, bro."

I didn't want to be a brother or any other member of his family, but I politely shook his hand, the one with the black glove.

Then I stared at Leslie; Leslie stared at Todd; Todd closed his eyes and made *do dah da do dah dah do* sounds: music. Eventually he grinned.

"Little song I'm writing called 'Don't Blame the Care Bears If You Step on Something in the Woods.' It's like satirical environmental funk." Then he carefully tested his hair. "Can we get some shade? It's hot out here."

"Not for Leslie," I said. "She never sweats. Never has. Never will."

He looked me over, frowned, grinned. "Right. Exactly. Never will, huh? Cool."

Leslie had that dazed look people get after Dracula's taken a couple of sips. So I pointed over my shoulder. "We might as well go in."

With Todd between us, we made our way through the crowd. Some people stared, a few frowned, and a girl in tight cycling shorts kept poking her girlfriend and pointing our way.

So Todd arranged his scarves for her and snarled. Or — which is closer to the truth, I guess — he let his tongue sort of roll out of his mouth. It looked to me like he'd just got a taste of old eggroll, but the girl was stoked.

He let Leslie slip ahead, then nudged me. "She could tell I'm in a band."

"Gee, and I thought you were a missionary."

I got his bandstand grin. "Man, that stuff never happened when I was wearing my fingers out on Bach transcriptions."

When he stopped to wave at another dazzled preteen, I whispered to Leslie, "Are you sure this is the right Todd?"

"No." She managed to grin. "Maybe it's just the clothes?"

Just then Todd waved good-bye to his fans, both arms high — a farewell-to-my-adoring-throng gesture I'd seen on MTV concert footage. Then he swooped down on Leslie again.

"Doesn't mean a thing, babe. Don't get jealous." One of his long arms draped over her shoulders.

"Who's jealous?" She pushed his hand away. "Why didn't you tell me about . . . you know?"

"I wanted it to be a suprise."

"A suprise? I almost had a heart attack. You don't look like yourself at all. Your hair is different. You're dressed different." She pushed at his sweaty, bare chest with her fingertips. "You're so skinny."

"Hey, don't let people tell you there's no politics in heavy metal. How can you make anarchy and disorder a trademark while you pig out at the pasta bar with the see-through sneeze shield?"

"But you looked so great. And you played so great. You sounded just like that guy you liked, that Andrés Segovia guy."

Todd stopped, took Leslie by the shoulders, and stared down at her. His earrings — a skull and a tiny Mickey Mouse — caught the light.

"Babe," he said shaking his head solemnly, "I was goin' nowhere in classical music. Nowhere. I was stuck."

"Are you kidding? You were good!"

"Yeah? Well, so what? I'd been taking lessons for how many years? Like nine." More head shaking. "I never told you this, Leslie, but I was livin' the life my folks wanted me to live, especially my dad. He's the one who wanted to see me up there with my foot on that stupid little stool. He's the one who had me playing at home while Mom served drinks." He looked over at me, then back. "I kept wondering when they were going to tip me."

He took one hand away, reached for his hair, then stopped himself. I'd seen my dad do that a million times. My dad. At least he didn't make me sit in the living room and play "She'll Be Comin' Round the Mountain" on my comb.

Todd sighed. "Anyway, one day after my eleven thousandth lesson, I go into Guitar City, remember? On Burgess Street?"

Leslie nodded, and I watched her look him over. Again. I knew what she was thinking, because I was thinking it, too: Where was the Todd she'd talked about so much, the one she wanted?

The one we had plowed on: "Anyway, I pick up a copy of *Rock & Roll Flash* that's lyin' there, right? And all of a sudden, there it is." When he blocked out the ad for us with one hand, I saw that he'd painted his fingernails black. Either that or he was a lousy carpenter.

"'Destroyers want guitar player. Need serious hair, desire, equipment. Outlaw image a must.' So I called."

"You looked like this already?" Leslie asked.

"No way. I was wearing Levi's Dockers. Those dudes about fell out of their Harley-Davidson T-shirts when I walked in." It was time to include me again, so his eyes swept my way like a lighthouse beam. "Then I started to play." The memory was so sweet, he raised both clenched fists over his head. "Leslie, I'm the youngest by about four years, and I'm carrying those guys. Guess what they know about music — three chords and how to turn up the amp."

Todd had gotten a little intense, sort of driving Leslie toward the guard's shack while I trailed along. So he took a deep breath, shook his hair — *carefully* shook his hair if that's possible — and rubbed his bare stomach. When he let his head fall back, both eyes closed slowly.

Like a doll's. *Ken surprises the entire Mattel organization with a new look!* Then he made soft guitar sounds: "*Thum, thum, ta dah, ta ta dah, ta ta dah.*"

Leslie looked at me. I shrugged. What could we do but listen? It sounded like "Paradise City," the old Guns 'n' Roses song. Finally she blurted out, "But what do your folks think?"

He grinned. "They hate it."

Then he showed me his perfect teeth, and I wondered if now he had to go to a dentist who wore a black sleeveless smock and an earring in his nose.

Poor Leslie was still looking clobbered. I flashed my stable pass and pointed. "C'mon," I said. "Let's show Todd around."

Back at the barns, Mitch and Donna got up off the bench by the office. I knew they'd been primed for this, and Mitch looked nervous, frowning and wiping his hands on his cords.

Leslie said, "Daddy, this is Todd, the boy I told you about from school? He's, uh, trying something, uh, different, for his, um, career."

Mitch stared like somebody'd brought him a deer to train. "Is this his costume? Is he in a play?"

Leslie groaned. "No, Daddy. He's a musician."

Todd took off his glove to shake hands. "I'm glad to meet you, sir," he said.

All of a sudden I could hear the nice kid in him. The kid his parents had raised. The kid Leslie had liked. Then we all stood around again, not looking at each other. Finally Donna asked, "How'd you get your hair to do that?"

Todd rolled his eyes up like somebody trying to see his own forehead.

"Oh, there's this place called The Wild Hair in Berkeley, where all the musicians go. They crank up the music real loud, and there's lots of girls and —" He caught himself. "Just girls who work there, Leslie. You know, shampoo girls and stuff." He swung back toward Donna. "When I went in the first time, I was scared to death. I had this real dorky pony tail."

"Your hair was nice," Leslie snapped, and she stomped away.

That made for another squirmy moment or two until Mitch half-turned toward the office and said, "Well, you all bump into me later, okay? I'll see if I can't find something to bet. Make Todd here enough money to get his hair done again."

Mitch wasn't trying to be mean, and Todd took it pretty well. He just nodded good-bye, then flashed me a little what-can-you-expect look.

We trooped away in a short safari line. It was like Leslie and I were leading Todd toward the Lost City of Gold Records. As we angled past most of Mitch's stock and headed for Pepperoni, Todd remarked, "They're like in prison, aren't they?"

It wasn't that original a thought, I guess, but somehow I didn't expect Todd to have it. I slowed a little and let him catch up. I also took in Leslie, with her back to us.

"Yeah," I said. "it is a little like that."

Leslie whirled around. She was wound up like a brand-new watch.

"They're taken good care of," she informed us in no uncertain terms.

"Sure, Todd said. "As long as they do what you want. As long as they're good little beasts of burden. You just better hope they never revolt."

"They're horses, Todd," I said. "They don't get together late at night and make bombs."

"*Dow de dow,*" he sang to himself. "*Dah do de dow.*" Then he started to croon, "The passive steeds need anarchy . . ." His eyes rolled up again. It made me wonder if he had some lyrics hidden in his bangs.

After what seemed like three weeks went by, I tried to help him out. "They need to think perpendicularly?"

His eyes, which had been half-closed, popped open: "Yes. All right, Graham." We exchanged soul-brother slaps.

"Don't you start, too," Leslie warned me.

Todd waggled his eyebrows, bleached to match his hair. "Hey, you told me Graham was cool."

"Can we just go see Pepperoni?"

Three abreast, we swept around the corner as Todd asked, "So are they all named after pizza?"

Leslie skidded, whirled around. "He's kidding, isn't he?" she asked me.

"C'mon, Leslie. How dumb do you think I am?"

Before she could answer that, I said, "Leslie knows the names of all her dad's horses, don't you, Les?"

"No, I don't," she said.

"Sure, you do."

Her lips were pressed together so tight they'd all but disappeared. "I don't remember all of them." She glanced at Todd. "My brain's been damaged by a recent shock."

"Aw, c'mon," I urged her. "Try."

"All right. All right." And she wiped both hands on her jeans like she was about to go up to bat with two out and two on. "Let's start with Mama Heart, then Road To Win, Chime Song, Airmail Special." She frowned, glanced at me, then remembered. "Oh, yeah, Hall's A Poppin', Mission Hills, Pepperoni, Holt On, Pretzel King, Tabled For Good, and Hot Line."

Todd's arms went around her, and I noticed she didn't fight so hard to stay away from him this time.

"That was cool, Les. I'm still usin' a crib sheet for song lyrics."

She held onto his vest with both hands. "It's a trick," she mumbled. "Graham taught me."

"Really?" Todd asked.

"It's no big deal." I shrugged. "I don't even know if it'd work for songs. But I can show you tonight if you want."

"Oh, yeah. Tonight." He adjusted his coat — or was it just the longest vest in the Western world — so that less of his pale chest showed. Leslie had to step back. "We'll see. Okay?"

We'd stopped in front of Pepperoni's stall. I was probably beaming like a proud parent. Todd even took off his shades.

"Wow! Is he a giant!"

"She."

"You're kidding. Queen of the Amazons." He put one hand out, and as Pepperoni nuzzled it, he grinned like a kid. "I wonder if her bones hurt."

Leslie and I whipped around. "What?"

"Hey, relax. I just said I wonder if her bones hurt because she's so big. I grew almost two inches this semester, and my bones were killing me. That's why my folks took me for X rays."

Maybe Todd should've picked another kind of rays, because suddenly Leslie was mad again. "I should've known then that you'd changed. Real classical guitarists don't send girls their stupid X rays."

I couldn't help myself. "What'd the doctor say?"

"Just to take it easy until the tendons and all the rest of that stuff caught up."

"Did it hurt when you ran?" I asked intently. "I mean, it didn't feel like anything was going to just come apart, did it?"

"Not exactly. It just hurt. Why?"

"Nothing. It's okay. Forget it."

Leslie stepped between us. She had more on her

mind than Pepperoni. "You really should have told me how different you were."

Todd whirled around in frustration, and his scarves billowed. "Like how? Send you a picture so you could dump on me, too?"

"I wouldn't have. I just —"

"Oh, really? Well, everybody else did. People from school. Teachers. My parents' friends. It was like I had leprosy all of a sudden." He twisted his hands like worried people do in the soaps. "'Oh, are you on drugs?' 'Should we consider family counseling?' 'You were always such a nice boy.'"

He faced us again. "What really went down, anyway? Did I quit school? No, I quit music lessons. Did I start smoking crack? No way. Drinking? Nada. What's really different? My clothes and, okay, my philosophy maybe. But I'm almost sixteen. I want to live my own life for a change." Some of the horses around us started to stir, so he brought his voice down. "You understand, don't you, Leslie?"

She was staring at her boots. "I don't know."

"Graham?"

"I think so."

Leslie leaned toward him and touched his hair. "It's not that I don't still like you, Todd. I'm just surprised."

Todd looked glum. "You don't have a clue about me."

Leslie was like a little fire that might've gone out if Todd hadn't kept blowing on it. She flicked one of his curls back at him, wiped her fingers on her jeans, and snapped, "How could I have a clue? You never told me! And, anyway, what would you think if I showed up after two months and I'd lost a ton of weight and bought some leather pants and wouldn't eat at salad bars anymore?"

"I hope I'd understand, okay?"

"Well, I'm trying to."

Todd sighed and flicked one of the silver conchas that ran up the seams of his pants.

Just then the stable loudspeaker called for horses. Leslie grabbed Todd's hand while I turned around and looked into Pepperoni's left eye.

"Don't worry," I whispered. "You don't need your pelvis x-rayed. You're perfect."

≡ ≡ ≡

We were halfway across the picnic area, maybe twenty yards from the escalators, when Todd said something to Leslie, then jogged ahead.

I hurried up beside her. "What now?" I asked.

"He just said to watch."

Well, it would have been hard not to watch, because all of a sudden Todd went into a rock-idol frenzy. He played air-guitar furiously, danced around till his scarves stood straight out, then ran toward us at top speed, dropped to his knees in the long grass, and slid right up to Leslie strumming his stomach, gritting his teeth, and spitting out, "*Da dah do dah do du dah do du dah.*"

She turned the deepest red I'd ever seen. I'll bet she was red clear through, like a tomato.

While everybody stared, Leslie gritted her teeth. "I have to go to the bathroom," she hissed. "For about a year." Then she took off. If Pepperoni could get out of the gate that fast, I'd have a lot less to worry about.

I led Todd up the escalator and we stood by the water fountain right next to the arrows that said MEN and WOMEN.

"How long is she gonna be?" he asked, brushing grass off his knees.

"She said a year, but I think we can be home for Christmas."

He rolled his eyes, as if the problem was Leslie. "Man, it took me two weeks and six pairs of pants to get that down. Every other girl in the world goes for those moves. What's the matter with her?"

"Nothing's the matter with her. For one thing —" But he wasn't listening. A few yards away, two sixteen-year-olds in tube tops checked him out, giggled, and whispered to each other.

"I can't have just one girlfriend, anyway, Graham. I mean look at me. I'm an outlaw now. And the drummer said outlaws have to go from babe to babe. Kind of like bees."

"Bees?"

"Yeah." His fingers skipped through the air. "Flower to flower." Then he pointed to the smoky grandstand, the long lines of people holding racing forms. "Plus I'm more out of it down here than she was up north, and believe me, she was out of it." This time he just went ahead and plowed his hand through his champagne-colored hair. "All that racetrack stuff. Nobody knew where she was coming from. The first time I saw her at school, I figured she was in a country-and-western band. I mean, she was wearing her cowboy hat inside! I started to talk to her because I thought she might play guitar." He checked behind him again. "Then before you know it she's crazy about me and those baroque pieces, especially the Scarlatti." For a moment he seemed almost wistful. Then he just redialed 1-800-I'M SO BAD. "But everything's different now. If nothin' else, I'm in Oakland, and she's in L.A. We're talking serious geographic undesirables."

"So are you gonna tell her all this?"

"I think she knows. Girls usually know."

"Listen, Todd. I think Leslie's gonna be glad to see you get back on that tram, but if you leave here tomorrow without telling her how things stand, I'll hunt you down and chew your fingers off."

He grimaced and put both hands behind his back. "Uh, look, about tomorrow. There's not gonna be one. I didn't fly down with my dad. I drove down with the band. The guys are gonna pick me up at four. We're jamming in Encinitas tonight. I was gonna take Leslie along, see. Stand her right down in front while we played. But not now — no way." He stared past me.

"And, anyhow, if the babes there are anything like the babes here . . ."

"You're a real creep, Todd, you know that?"

"Hey, lighten up, okay? I'm gonna tell her. I'm just waitin' for the right time."

I spotted Leslie then and nudged him. She'd washed her face, and there were only a couple of embarrassed spots left high on each cheek, like faded clown makeup.

"Would either of you like a snack?" she asked, sounding like she'd met Miss Manners in the girls' room.

"I guess," Todd said. "Sure."

"You guys go ahead. You haven't had any time alone yet." I glared at Todd. "Maybe one of you wants to tell the other one something important."

My parents had gone home, so I went and sat in the empty box and studied a racing form Dad had left behind. His figures, in different-colored inks, were scrawled beside the horses he liked.

Then I felt somebody behind me.

"Are you keeping an eye on things for me?" Mitch asked, leaning down.

"Uh-huh."

"Did you all go by Pepperoni's stall on your way up here?"

"She's fine. If Todd didn't scare her, I don't see why a starting gate would."

Mitch punched me good-naturedly. "Well, tell that poor man's Mick Jagger to bet on Over Easy in this race." He looked toward the infield and the flashing lights of the tote board. "He won't pay much, but he ought to win."

As he left, I heard Leslie say, "Hi, Daddy," and then a Coke appeared over my shoulder. I took a sip and asked, "Where's Todd? Another photo opportunity for his clamoring fans?"

"He got in the hot dog line."

"That should be appetizing. He's so skinny it'll probably show, like on *Wild Kingdom* when the skunk snake eats the poor little mouse and then there's this gross bulge."

Leslie squinted, then tugged at her lucky hat, the tall one with the red and black beadwork on the band. "What's wrong with you all of a sudden?"

I held up the Coke. "When you were in line for this, what'd you talk about?"

Shrug. "Not much. Except that he was sorry he embarrassed me by sliding around on the grass."

"That's all?"

"A couple of girls in shorts came by and wanted to know what band he was in."

Then Todd came back and vaulted into the seat beside Leslie. "Great hot dog," he said, patting his stomach.

"Spare me, okay? Button your vest."

He rubbed his hands together. "So, who do we bet on?"

She showed him her program. Almost immediately he breathed a long "Wow," the kind of sound you'd make after opening up a trunk and finding gold. He pointed to the number five horse. "Hendrix, man."

"We know that horse," said Leslie.

It was my turn to point and to lean across Leslie. "Mitch said to use Over Easy. Hendrix isn't much of a runner."

"No, no, you don't understand." Todd tapped the program. "Hen-drix." He pronounced both syllables slowly like he was teaching immigrants the history of rock 'n' roll. "He was the greatest guitar player that ever lived."

"I know who he is. I saw the Woodstock documentary. But so what?"

"Oh, man." Todd fell back in his seat and sighed — Born to Be Misunderstood. "Ever hear of synchronicity? Dig it, okay: Hendrix is a guitar player; I'm a guitar player. I'm at the track; he's at the track."

"Hendrix is a horse, Todd. He lives at the track. It'd only be synchronicity if he showed up at your concert."

"You don't get it, man."

"I don't get it? Hendrix is seventy to one. Don't tell me who doesn't get it."

"Todd," Leslie said patiently. "Look at this racing form, okay? This shows how Hendrix has been running lately. It's like his history and —"

"History? Leslie, history is what the media-poisoners tell us it is. It's edited. You don't think you're getting all the facts there, do you?"

I tried to stay calm. "Todd, this isn't the L.A. Times. It's a racing paper."

"Man, I thought you two were hipper than that. I thought —"

"Take his money, Leslie."

They both looked at me.

"Take his money, and give it to Mitch to bet. He's not gonna listen to logic."

Todd nodded. "'Cause logic is bull." He tapped his chest with its two lonely hairs. "Trusting yourself is what matters." He stared at the flashing numbers. "So what does seventy mean?"

Leslie explained that it meant for every dollar bet you get back seventy. "But the minimum's two dollars, so that's a hundred and forty."

"And what if I plunk down twenty?"

"Over a thousand," I told him.

"*Ahhwooo!*" He gave one of those jungle cries and stamped his booties gleefully. "And that's exactly what I need to buy a new Kramer. Don't you see how this all fits together? Don't you see how perfect it is?"

I reached into my pocket. "Mitch said to use Over Easy; he's also got the big number on my dad's form. Six to win, okay?"

Todd dug into an almost nonexistent pocket of his skintight pants. "All of it," he said, waving a crumpled bill.

As Leslie said, "I'll be right back" and patted us both good-bye, Todd started to play his invisible guitar again, but I grabbed his right hand. And squeezed.

"I'll tell her!" He shook free and massaged his wrist. "Jeez, Teen Enforcer."

Five minutes later, when the horses broke, Todd stood up and started to scream. "Yes, Jimi. Yes, my man. Hendrix. Hendrix. Yes! Yes! Yes!" He had both arms up like a football referee. His eyes were closed.

It takes a lot to distract gamblers, but Todd did it, chanting at the top of his lungs like a long-distance guru. And he kept it up until Leslie tugged at him. Then when he wouldn't quit, she just pushed him back into his seat. People were staring. People we'd known for years, staring and frowning like we were eating off the flag.

"The race is over, Todd! For God's sake, shut up!"

"What happened?" he said, looking dazed.

"You lost," I told him. "By the usual twenty lengths. And I won."

"You're kidding."

Leslie said that I wasn't.

"I didn't know who to watch. They're all the same color."

"Their numbers are different, though." I showed him my ticket. "Mine's on the board. Yours isn't."

He stood up. "I can't believe it. That was all the money I had." He glanced at Leslie and me. "I'm really bummed." Todd dropped his head, spraddled his legs, and started making down-and-dirty guitar sounds and strumming his ribs:

"Got the Mariposa blues; I'm as blue as I can be."

The funny thing was that he could really sing. I mean he sounded good. A few people stopped to listen as he snuck a glance at me out of one corner of his eye.

"Got the Mariposa blues; I'm as blue as I can be.
This whole trip turned out to be a big catastrophe."

Then he changed imaginary chords, stood up, and took it from the top. That got him a little hand on the last long, soulful note.

Then he took Leslie's hand. "Walk with me, okay?"

She looked suprised. "Where?"

"Doesn't matter. By the entrance, maybe." He glanced my way. "There's something I want to tell you."

≡ ≡ ≡

Outside the gates, just down from where we'd met him at one o'clock, Todd waved to some guys sitting in a white Volvo station wagon. Then he turned around, draped his arms over Leslie's shoulders, and leaned in, putting his forehead against hers like he was going to break the news by osmosis.

I stood a few yards away. Everybody else in his band had their shades on and their hair down and their vests open. But the Volvo had to belong to one of their parents. Its personalized license plate said WAGGIN — way too uncool for outlaw anarchists.

I tried to keep my eyes to myself, but I saw Leslie slump. I watched him slide his hands down to her waist just before he kissed her. Or she kissed him. Anyhow, they kissed. When she pulled herself away and started toward me, I could see she was pale and her face was all scrunched up.

Then Todd yelled, "Graham! What was that rhyme you made up after 'The passive steeds need anarchy'?"

For a second I didn't know what he was talking about. Then I remembered his impromtu song in the barn.

"Go buzz around Encinitas," I said.

"Aw, c'mon." He pointed at Leslie's back. "I did what you said, didn't I?"

I could hear her boots behind me, retreating.

"Something about needing to think perpendicularly, okay? Now get out of here!"

He saluted with a clenched fist and got into the Volvo. I heard the car pull away as I hurried to catch up with Leslie. She tore down the frontage road like she was really going somewhere. Finally, I took hold of her elbow, and that seemed to set her off.

"I hate him," she choked. "I hate him so much." Her breath was coming fast and shallow the way it does just before you cry. "How could I have ever liked him?"

"He changed," I said. "He wasn't the same guy that you told me about at all."

"He kept calling me babe like I was some kind of blue ox." She sniffed. "And he didn't even want to stay for dinner. Not that I wanted him to. I wanted him to just hurry up and get out of here and go back to all the groupie shampoo girls or whatever."

"What'd he say, anyway?"

"Just that he was some kind of bee."

"Well, you still kissed him good-bye for a pretty long time."

"I just wanted to make sure I hated him as much as I thought. Even his lips were skinny. It was like kissing a snake. And, anyway, you should talk; you helped him write a song."

I took off my straw hat and rubbed my head, something Dad always did when he was frustrated.

"Let's don't you and me fight, okay?" We weren't that far from the stable entrance that faced the ocean, a quarter of a mile away. I angled her that way. "I mean, he's gone now. It's over."

Leslie stopped, took off her hat, and leaned into my white shirt. "Damn it, Graham. I was really looking forward to today. I had this idea, this stupid fantasy. I thought . . ."

She was crying hard, and Leslie didn't cry much. I'd seen her thrown off a horse, then just get up and cuss. So I patted her shoulder a little, but she twisted away, keeping her face hidden.

When she let up a little, I got her moving again. "Well, at least with Todd here I wasn't thinking about tomorrow. And what could happen to Pepperoni. It made me nervous when he said logic was bull and you had to trust your feelings. That's what I did with Pepperoni. That's how I got in this mess."

"I wouldn't believe anything he said. Ever."

We just walked then for a little bit while Leslie took deep breaths and sniffed. When we got close to the barns I said, "Look, why don't you come and eat with us tonight?"

"With you and your folks?"

I grinned. "No, with me and Pepperoni. We're having carrot casserole and an oat loaf."

Leslie grinned for the first time in a while. Then she leaned away to spit. "Did you ask your mom about this?"

"She won't care. Has she ever cared?"

"Okay. I'll call home from your place."

$$\equiv \quad \equiv \quad \equiv$$

The next afternoon, I got to the track a little late so I wouldn't have too much time to think. First, I swung by Mitch's barn and slipped into Pepperoni's stall. I hunkered down, pushed aside the clean straw Leslie and I'd thrown in that morning, and felt her ankles — cool as fish. Then I ran both hands over her neck and sides. Finally I reached for the halter, clucked at her, and put my forehead against her nose.

"Take it easy out there today," I said. "There's a long race in a few weeks I bet you can win. And lots more next year and the year after that. You just lope along and finish in one piece, okay?"

I kissed her on the nose, ducked so she wouldn't kiss me back — not with *those* humongous lips — then handed her over to Donna. Finally I hiked the quarter of a mile over to the walking ring, taking deep breaths all the way and wishing I had a 7-Up.

With just fifteen minutes to the post, it was crowded.

Pepperoni was last in, and Leslie and I both waved to Donna as the horses and their handlers arranged themselves like the numbers on a clock.

"So far so good," Leslie said, without taking her eyes off the filly.

"For her, maybe. I threw up this morning."

"You're just nervous."

"Thank you, doctor."

As the horses circled us, DiFiero's friends flitted around. DiFiero even stopped and shook hands with Leslie and me. His hand was soft and white like Wonder bread.

"Are you okay?" I asked Leslie as Mitch talked to the jockey. "You didn't say two words to me all morning."

"I'm okay. Better, anyway. I took a walk while you were surfing, and then I talked to Donna a little."

"What'd she say?"

We watched a light-boned bay go upon her hind legs, and everybody but her groom scuttled out of the way.

"I'll tell you later. Mostly I figured it out for myself: shoot, the Todd I want's not sleepin' it off in Encinitas this morning. The Todd I want's up north someplace, or" — she pointed to her head — "up here."

I put my arm around her as Mitch gave his rider a leg up. Then we watched the field file out through the gauntlet of chattering, anxious fans.

Five minutes later I was sitting beside Leslie, pitched forward with my forehead against the back of the seat in front of me. I honestly thought I was going to have to start breathing into a paper bag.

"How does she look?" I asked, staring down at the torn tickets, gum wrappers, and napkins.

"Graham, you just saw her in the paddock."

""Yeah, but I thought I'd pass out up here where everybody could see. Is she lathered anywhere?"

"Dry as a bone." I felt Leslie's hand on the back of my lucky shirt. "She likes it out there, Graham. Look at her."

"I can't. What's the rider doing?"

"I'm not sure, but he's got a cellular phone and a catalog. Maybe he's ordering some jockey shorts."

I glanced up. "That's the kind of dumb thing Todd would've said."

"Go ahead. Be mean to your only friend in the world."

"Oh, God. She stopped."

"Relax, Graham."

"I thought you told me to look at her."

"I was wrong. Sit back down and stare at the concrete."

"Something's wrong. She's not moving at all. I'll bet she's paralyzed. She won't even be able to hobble into the ambulance. They'll have to bring in a crane."

Leslie stood beside me. "She is so smart." Calmly, she nodded toward Pepperoni. The jockey had given her some rein, and she was looking things over: the noisy stands, the people at the rail, the infield lagoons. Then, satisifed, she jogged on.

Leslie had a hold of my hand so tight it hurt.

"She's the only horse in the race that took the time to get her bearings like that."

"It doesn't mean she won't get hurt."

A big frown. "You are startin' to make *me* nervous."

"How much time to the race?" I asked.

"Ten minutes."

"I can't sit here for that long. I'll throw up again."

"You've convinced me. Let's go somewhere else."

We ended up leaning against the white fence around the deserted saddling paddock. The odds board showed Pepperoni at thirteen to one.

"Thirteen," I said. "That's not good."

"Graham. Somebody's got to be thirteen. It just means if she wins she pays twenty-six dollars. That's all it means."

"All right. I prayed for Pepperoni last night."

"You didn't do anything stupid, did you, like promise to eat beets for the rest of your life if she won?"

"Didn't you pray?" I demanded.

"Just that all of Todd's hair would fall out by this morning."

"Five minutes, folks," said the announcer.

I glanced at the odds board — Now she was fourteen to one. That was better.

"Graham? I'll tell you what Donna said about Todd and me, okay? Are you listening? She said that he was crazy to dump somebody like me. And she liked it that I told him he kissed like a snake. Then she said that even though I got hurt a little, now I was like the horses in the racing form. I had a history, and the comment on my past performance with Todd would read like this: 'Promising debut. Filly with a future.'"

I looked at her blue eyes, the color of Pepperoni's silks. "You told him that he kissed like a snake?"

"You bet."

"Well, all right!"

"Good." She patted me briskly. "That's more like it. You sound almost human again."

Just then the announcer boomed, "They're at the post! For the Solo Chico Stakes."

I held out my hand. "Oh, man. What if I was wrong?"

She wove her fingers through mine. "You're not gonna be wrong!"

$$\equiv \quad \equiv \quad \equiv$$

Pepperoni broke with her field, then dropped back to almost last. Leslie patted my arm before I could panic. "We knew she might do that."

I took a turn with the binoculars. Horses might look like jackrabbits when they shoot out of the gate, but when they run they don't push with their back legs so much as they pull with their front ones, the really fragile ones. So I started there and worked my way back.

"She's fine," I hollered at Leslie.

Leslie shouted back. "I said she was fine."

I was numb all over and held the glasses tight so they wouldn't slip out of my hands, which felt like big paws. Mitch pointed, and DiFiero frowned. My dad leaned forward, both hands around the back of the seat in front of him.

When they turned for home, the jockey got her outside, hit her left-handed a couple of times, and she started to run. But way too late. She closed to be a distant fourth, ten lengths behind the winner.

The whole race didn't last much more than a minute. I'd held my breath the whole time.

"She made it!" Leslie bellowed. "I knew she would."

Even while Leslie tugged on my arm, I told her to wait, and I climbed up on the seat to follow Pepperoni around the clubhouse turn. It wasn't until she slowed down and started to gallop back that I relaxed.

Mitch was pointing, holding both hands out like a fisherman to show how much she'd win by once she stretched out, and DiFiero was nodding. Mom had turned all the way around to grin at me.

"Look at that," said Leslie as the jockey pulled Pepperoni up by the judges' stand and slid off. "She's not breathin' hard enough to blow out a match."

I sat down. Man, was I beat. Could I do this for a living? I'd need thousands of dollars worth of nerve tonic and deodorant.

Just then Mitch came by to collect Leslie because we had a horse in the nightcap. He shook my hand.

"She closed like an express train," he drawled. "She'll get there next time."

I got up to go with them, but Mitch pushed me back in my seat. "Stay right there. You've had enough excitement for one day."

Leslie leaned over me. "You were right!" she said. "You were right all along. You should be proud of yourself."

"Okay," I croaked.

Then she playfully flipped my hat forward and skipped away.

That was when my dad made his way back to me, turning sideways to get between people gathering up their stuff after a long day at the races.

"Want a Coke?" he asked, offering me a red and white cup.

"Sure."

But I just held it until he frowned and said, "It's a new one. I didn't drink out of it or anything."

I took a quick sip. "It's not that. I'm just a little knocked out."

Down on the track, Donna was leading Pepperoni away. Dad looked at her for a long time. Finally he said, "I'm glad things worked out the way they did."

"Me, too. I was worried for a while."

He shook his head. "You were right about her, though, and you stuck to your guns."

I sighed and looked at him. I mean really *looked* at

him. "The thing is that it was like the deepest feeling I ever had. You can't be a trainer with one stupendous hunch every fourteen years."

He reached for the Coke and took a swallow. "You're young, Graham. Take your time with this, okay?"

Just then a few people got up, and I heard the growl of a tractor. Dad turned around. I stood on my tiptoes, careful not to lean against him.

"The six horse," he said, holding his program so I could see.

She couldn't put any weight on her right front, so her handler hadn't been able to lead her back to the barn.

My dad stared, frowning. Other people looked away; some focused their binoculars; some just opened up their racing newspapers and hid behind them.

As the horse ambulance swept up, I said, "That could've been Pepperoni."

Dad was firm. "But it wasn't. That's the point."

"Seems to me the point is I wasn't so much right as I was just lucky."

"Why don't we say you were both."

Out of the corner of my eye, I saw the white ambulance pull away. My father reached for my hat, angling it first one way, then another. He was kidding around now. Or trying to.

"Are you hungry?" he asked.

"Probably."

"Well, let's bet this last race and then go out to dinner,

have a little celebration." He opened up his racing form. "I like the four."

I shook my head and pointed to my program.

"Not Mitch's horse!" he exclaimed.

"Uh-huh."

"That thing can't run, Graham."

"You don't know that."

"The hell I don't!"

"Oh, c'mon. Leslie and I worked on him every day, and he looks great."

"And what's that supposed to mean, that Mitch is a better trainer than I am?"

I glanced down and noticed I'd twisted my program into a wick. Dad took off his hat and rubbed his head.

"The hair doctor said to not do that," I reminded him.

"Don't you start, too, kiddo."

I watched the neon lights on the tote board change. Mitch's horse was eleven to one. Dad was grinding his teeth again.

"The price is right," I ventured.

"It's a sucker bet," he snapped.

I waited until some people angled past us before I asked, "Are we gonna argue about everything forever?"

"I don't know about forever, but for sure we are when you want to throw good money away on slow horses."

I started to get red in the face again. "That's not true. That's not hardly it at all. It's about more than horses.

You just want me to agree with you about everything, don't you?"

He frowned so hard his eyebrows came together, and he looked me up and down like I was a stranger. The funny thing is that we were dressed alike: black roper's boots, jeans, white shirts.

"Your mother," he said, quieter than I expected, "told me you and I'd start to argue."

I looked toward my mom who was reading again. Her right arm, the one that had curled around me a million times, rested on the back of the nearest seat. Her red hair glowed like a campfire. "I argue with Mom, too." Then I quoted her, "'I'm an equal opportunity brat.'"

He reached out to touch my shoulder, but carefully, like I was a painting or a cake. "You're a lot like her."

"I guess, but I'm like you, too."

Dad's eyes narrowed. "Is that bad?"

"No, not anymore." The words were barely out of my mouth when I realized I meant it.

He took a big breath, let it out, and glanced at his program, then back at me. "I've been thinking lately about how when you were little I really wanted things to be different for you than they were for me." He was frowning, picking out his words carefully, like choosing coins from a deep pocket. Coins that had to add up just right. "And I thought they *were* different because you never had to go without like I did. And that counts some. But, you know, the fact is sometimes I hear myself crabbing at you or arguing with you or telling you to do something that you don't want to do, and it's almost me and my dad all over again."

"Did you ever give him as hard a time as I've been giving you this summer?"

"Harder." He raised both eyebrows. "Interesting in a way, isn't it?"

"Yeah."

Just then the guy on the public address system warned us not to get shut out.

"So are we gonna bet?" he asked.

"What about if just you and I each pick a horse and forget about the rest of the race. One of us is bound to finish in front of the other, even if we run last and second-last."

"I'm not about to run second-last, but let's say we did it your way. Then what?"

"Loser buys dinner. For Leslie and Donna and Mitch, too. Okay?"

"Can you afford to pay for six people?"

"I'm not gonna lose, but I've got money. Enough for dinner, anyway."

"I guess you do at that."

The announcer, for the last time that day, boomed, "Post time!"

Dad looked around. "C'mon. Let's sit down so people can see."

He motioned for me to go ahead then, and all the way to the seats I could feel his hand on my shoulder, guiding me. But so lightly I barely knew it was there.

East Union High School
Library
Manteca Unified School District

RON KOERTGE is the author of five books for young people including THE ARIZONA KID. He is a published poet and professor of English at Pasadena College. He lives in Pasadena with his wife, Bianca. When he's not at home he's most likely at the racetrack.